This book belongs to:

Be Bad

PRAISE FOR VILLAINS ACADEMY

'A charmingly villainous adventure about
friendship, school and unspeakable evil.'
Louie Stowell, author of *Loki: A Bad God's Guide to Being Good*

'Frightfully fun – *Villains Academy* had me
cackling from the very first page!'
Katie Tsang, co-author of the Dragon Realm series

'A joyful hug of a book with genuine warmth and heart.'
Hannah Gold, author of *The Last Bear*

'I loved the spookily funny *Villains Academy*.
It's a work of (evil) genius!'
Jenny McLachlan, author of *The Land of Roar*

'Criminally fun!'
Danny Wallace, author of *The Day the Screens Went Blank*

'Heart-warming and hilarious – *Villains Academy* is a spookalicious
treat, set to terrify every other book on your shelf.'
Jack Meggitt-Phillips, author of *The Beast and the Bethany*

'An absolute HOOT! Evil laughs aplenty!'
Sophy Henn, author and illustrator of the Pizazz series

'A delightfully fun adventure with real heart and humour.'
Benjamin Dean, author of *Me, My Dad and the End of the Rainbow*

'Immersive, funny, and with a cast of scarily loveable characters,
Villains Academy made me feel like I was IN the book!'
Mel Taylor-Bessent, author of *The Christmas Carrolls*

'This is a brilliant, bonkers work packed with top-notch illustration.'
Jack Noel, author and illustrator of the Comic Classics series

'Full of wonderful characters, *Villains Academy* is such a FUN read!'
Rikin Parekh, illustrator of The Worst Class in the World series

First published in Great Britain in 2023 by Simon & Schuster UK Ltd

Copyright © 2023 Ryan Hammond ← *Big bum!*

1 3 5 7 9 10 8 6 4 2

Dragons DO have bums!

Simon & Schuster UK Ltd ←
1st Floor, 222 Gray's Inn Road
London WC1X 8HB

Villains of the year!

www.simonandschuster.co.uk
www.simonandschuster.com.au
www.simonandschuster.co.in

Simon & Schuster Australia, Sydney
Simon & Schuster India, New Delhi

A CIP catalogue record for this book
is available from the British Library.

PB ISBN 978-1-3985-1464-5
eBook ISBN 978-1-3985-1465-2
eAudio ISBN 978-1-3985-1466-9

Hi, Sonny Peep.

Printed and bound by CPI Group (UK) Ltd,
Croydon, CR0 4YY

FSC
www.fsc.org

MIX
Paper from
responsible sources
FSC® C171272

SHEILA WAS ERE! :)

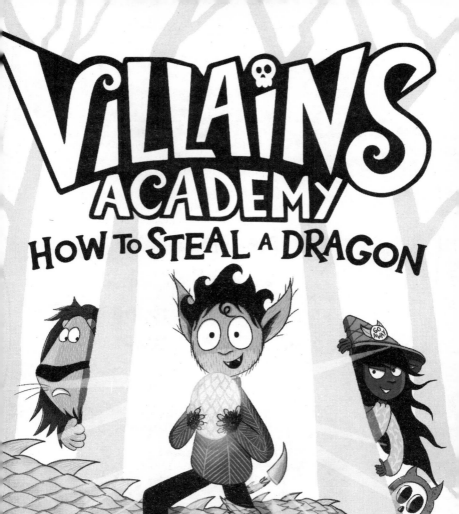

VILLAINS ACADEMY
HOW TO STEAL A DRAGON

Written, illustrated and designed by

RYAN HAMMOND

SIMON AND SCHUSTER

For Jamie.
My twin brother, best
friend and all-round
SHUBBLEMEGUMP!
x

CHAPTER 1
A HISTORY OF DRAGONS

'Dragons *do* have bums, sonny peep,' Sheila the ghost insisted.

'No, they don't, Sheila. We've gone over this before. None of us have ever seen a dragon's bum,' Skele-tony Le Bone replied, looking to his friends for support.

'But if they didn't have a bum, they'd blow up, so you're wrong,' Sheila said stubbornly.

☠ 1 ☠

'Then where's your bum, Sheila?' asked Mona, the elf-witch, looking the ghost up and down.

Sheila gasped dramatically. 'You can't just ask a lady where her bum is!'

Bram, the werewolf, laughed at the conversation that his friends, the Cereal Killers, were having. Well, three of them, minus Bryan the Lion, who was 'resting his eyes' before their lesson started and was letting off small toots in his sleep.

Two months ago, Bram had enrolled at the world-famous Villains Academy, a school for fledgling villains to learn all about being *bad*. In his first lesson, Bram was grouped together with Mona, Sheila, Tony and Bryan, and they quickly became known as the Cereal Killers. At the end of Bram's first week, the group had competed together in a challenge called the Mystery Maze where he came face to face with a ginormous dragon and

went on to win the coveted

VILLAIN OF
THE WEEK

title – a reward for the *baddest* student of the week, based on their performance throughout their lessons.

Ever since the Mystery Maze, Sheila had been trying to convince her friends that the dragon they'd met had a massive bazooma on its rear end.

'That's a *very* interesting observation, Mona. Do you have a bum, Tony?' Bryan asked as his eyes peeked open from his cat nap. 'Or do you lose it when you become a skeleton?'

Tony shook his head and removed his arm from its socket before wielding it like a weapon – something he often did to prepare for a fight. 'Yes, I do have a bum, so mind your own business. Speaking of which, here comes the biggest bum of them all.'

As if on cue, Master Mardybum, Class Z's form tutor, sauntered into the classroom. He was responsible for guiding them through their years at Villains Academy, as well as teaching the Poisons and Physical Escape classes, and he was known for being a tough nut to crack. 'Good morning, senseless nitwits. And what a wonderful day it is too!'

Behind him, a mysterious-looking man drifted quietly into the classroom

as if he were a ghost. His feet made no sound, but small flecks of frost appeared on the floorboards underfoot. His skin was as pale as snow, and his eyes pierced the room with their icy blue gaze, almost burning right into the fledgling villains' souls. His hair was as white as frost, and he wore a dazzling gown that shimmered with snowflakes.

'This is Felix Frostbite,' Master Mardybum announced. 'He's a fellow villain who will be teaching at the school from now on. He should have joined us at the start of term, like the rest of us poor teachers, but he was too busy gallivanting around the world being evil. His lessons will cover everything you need to know about ghastly beasts, but his speciality is dragons.'

At the mention of dragons, Class Z sat

up straight, their full attention now on the mysterious stranger. The Cereal Killers' rivals, the Overlords, could barely contain their excitement. Mal poised his pen above his notebook, Spike the Crocodile snapped his jaws at Jeeves the Cat to stop him cleaning himself, Mr Toad licked his lips menacingly and the Tooth Hairy's eyes looked like they were going to bulge out of her head. Even Bram's fur tingled at the thought of

learning about the ancient and mysterious creatures of evil.

'Have you ever ridden a dragon?' Mal shouted.

Felix Frostbite nodded with a cocky grin. 'I have. Dragons don't just let *anyone* ride them, though. Only the *baddest* villains are allowed on their backs, and few have succeeded, but I'm one of them,' he boasted.

Mona rolled her eyes, clearly not impressed by the teacher's arrogance.

Frostbite continued, 'You see, dragons are drawn to badness. If you join the Winter Warts, my exclusive club that promises to teach you how to be like me, a dragon master, you'll learn much more. Application forms will be left outside the food hall shortly.

My Ghastly Beasts lessons won't cover anything to do with dragons, so the Winter Warts is the place to go. Thank you, Master Mardybum, for introducing me. A pleasure to meet Class Z. I'll see you all after lunch for my first lesson. Toodles.'

Master Mardybum blushed, and Bram could have sworn that he saw his feet do a little skip under his robes. Was he . . . fangirling? Bram forced himself to look down at his desk in fear of bursting into laughter.

'No problem at all, Felix.' Master Mardybum swooned as the other teacher left the room without so much as a backwards glance. 'What a *dreadful* term it's going to be, Class Z! Now, on to today's lesson—'

'Sir!' Mr Toad interrupted as his hand

shot into the air. 'Are we going to get to ride a dragon?'

'What have I told you all – *don't* raise your hand in my classroom. Manners are not welcome here.' Master Mardybum frowned. 'And don't be so silly! No dragon would ever let you or anyone else here ride it. You're all too weak, foolish and young – especially you, Bram.'

Bram glared at his teacher in frustration. He'd won the Villain of the Week title on his very first week, and yet Master Mardybum still relished picking on him. Bram took a deep breath. 'You never know, we might surprise you. We did in the Mystery Maze after all.'

Master Mardybum waved him away with a swish of his enormous sleeve. 'Today isn't about dragons—'

'How many dragons are in the Wicked Woods?' the Tooth Hairy yelled, cutting the teacher off mid-sentence.

Master Mardybum sighed in irritation. 'We have the largest flight of dragons in the world living in the Wicked Woods. The school has had an agreement with them for centuries. We leave them to roam the woods in peace, and in return they protect our borders from incoming attacks.'

'Attacks?!' the Tooth Hairy exclaimed. 'Who would want to attack Villains Academy?'

'Heroes. Fellow villains that want to claim the world as their own. Wandering strangers. The list is endless. I daresay, without the dragons protecting us, Villains Academy would not exist. It would have been overrun and destroyed by our envious enemies a long time ago.' Master Mardybum grimaced. 'Now, the next person that asks me about dragons will be fed to them for dinner. Understood?' Master Mardybum's eyes began to glow with menace.

The class stayed silent.

'Peace at last.' The teacher smiled. 'We've got a lot to cover over the next couple of months, and there will be an exam at the end of term to test your knowledge. If you fail, you will be banned from attending the famous Villains Academy Blizzard Bash!'

A buzz of excitement vibrated through the air. The Blizzard Bash was an annual celebration at the end of the winter term, and it was rumoured to be the best party of the year!

'Trust me, you don't want to miss it,' Master Mardybum continued. 'So, to get you warmed up for today's lesson in disarming, we'll start with some simple dancing.'

'*Dancing*?' Sheila squealed.

The class looked at each other in horror. Mona slid so low in her chair that you could only see her hat with the GO AWAY badge peeking out above the desk, and Bram sat as still as possible, hoping to turn invisible.

'That's right!' Master Mardybum replied. 'You'll need to be able to defeat your peers on the dance floor at the Blizzard Bash, and the flexibility and agility training won't do you any harm for future combat. Wait until you see my

Deadly Dips, Horrendous High Kicks
and Bludgeoning Back Flips!'

'Ridiculous,' Mona moaned.

FAB-U-LOUS!' Sheila shouted.

'Have you seen my Toxic Tail Swish?
Years ago, I almost took my pal Janice's
eye out with it. I can demonstrate for
you now, if you like?'

'That won't be necessary, Sheila,'
Master Mardybum jumped in before
Sheila demolished everyone's eyeballs.
'Leave the dancing and teaching to me.
Now, I'd like you to divide into pairs and
I'll show you how to do a Deadly Dip.'

There was a collective groan, followed

by a scuffle of movement as everyone rushed to find a partner. Behind them, the classroom door slammed shut as Mona slipped out, claiming to have a sudden illness called Rotten Rumba.

Bram tried to follow her but was swept up by a waltzing Master Mardybum who threatened to tackle him to the floor if he moved another centimetre closer to the door. Bram held back tears of pain and reluctantly agreed to stay.

'Now it appears that everyone has a partner . . . apart from you, Bram.'

'I'll sit this one out, then.' Bram shrugged in relief, not wanting to make a fool of himself anyway.

'No chance! You'll just have to dance with me,' the teacher replied as he grabbed Bram's paw and whisked him around the classroom.

Bram felt his fur grow hot and he cringed, knowing his friends would never let him live this down. As if his weak villain instincts weren't embarrassing enough, now he had to dance with his *teacher*. He swore he could already hear Sheila whispering 'MardyBram' across the room.

'Don't you *dare* step on my gown,' Master Mardybum threatened. 'Right, Class Z, let's Deadly Dip.'

CHAPTER 2

THE WINTER WARTS

'How's your back?' Tony asked as Bram attempted to stretch. 'I know a good cracking technique if you need one.'

'I'll pass, thank you,' Bram replied. 'I didn't expect Master Mardybum to slam me to the ground like that. I thought we were *dancing*, not wrestling.'

The Cereal Killers sat round a table in the food hall eating their lunch of slimy sausage sandwiches – the slime being a mountain of ketchup that made Bryan look like a vampire. Even Mona had joined them to eat, having miraculously recovered from her unexpected sickness.

'It sounds horrendous,' she said. 'Though I would have liked to see you be body-slammed by Master Mardybum, Bram.'

'Ha ha,' Bram said sarcastically. 'You escaped this time, Mona, but you won't escape the Blizzard Bash. What's so bad about dancing anyway? Are you *embarrassed*?'

'I am *not* embarrassed,' Mona replied, suddenly becoming flustered. 'I don't like to dance. It's silly, and I'm not very good at it. Now, can we talk about something else, please?'

'Yes!' Sheila gasped. 'What about the new teacher, Felix Frostbite? Isn't he so *mysterious* and *cool*?'

'I wish my cape was as stylish as his gown,' Tony said, wiping ketchup off his sleeve.

'Mmm hmm,' Bryan mumbled, his mouth full of food.

Mona rolled her eyes. 'Well, I think he's big-headed and full of himself. Something about him doesn't sit right with me.'

Bram didn't know what to think. He couldn't judge Felix Frostbite on first impressions. If everyone had

done that with him when he started
at Villains Academy, he'd be known as
the nervous wreck who kept shouting,
'**BUMBERSHINS!**'
spontaneously.

'You silly sausage, Mona!' Sheila
replied and inhaled her final sausage in
one gulp. 'He's a supervillain! I think
we should definitely all join the Winter
Warts so we can ride dragons!'

'YES!' Tony and Bryan agreed in
unison.

Mona shrugged, not wanting to let on
how excited she was by the idea.

'I'm up for it.' Bram wanted to fly
a dragon more than anything. He just
hoped he'd be *bad* enough to be able to.
Winning the Mystery Maze was one
thing but persuading a dragon to let you
fly it was a whole other story, even with

his newfound courage.

'And we've got the Blizzard Bash to think about too! Who's everyone going with? And what are you all going to wear?' Tony asked excitedly.

'My birthday suit! I can't wait!' Sheila screeched. 'Tony, would you like to go with me?'

Tony grinned as if all his Christmases had come at once. 'Oh, yes! It would be my honour.'

Sheila leant towards Bram and whispered in his ear. 'He's the only one whose eyes I can't take out with my Toxic Tail Swish.'

Bram smiled, but his brain started to whirr with worry. He hadn't realized they'd have to *ask* people to the dance. What would happen if nobody wanted to go with him? Would he have to dance with Master Mardybum again? A chill travelled down his spine.

'Why don't we go as a group?' Bram suggested. 'The Cereal Killers together again, like in the Mystery Maze!'

'Don't be such a bore, Bram,' Bryan said as he finished licking the last drops of ketchup off his plate. 'I'm going to have people queuing up to accompany me. Although I might just go alone. You don't need a partner to have fun.'

But Bram didn't want to go alone. That would be embarrassing. Even *more* embarrassing than almost being thrown out of Villains Academy in his first week for allegedly stealing Furyflumps – squishy fruits that were said to make you extra *evil*, but in reality only gave you terrible wind.

It turned out that the pupils stealing Furyflumps had been Bryan, Sheila and Tony, which had caused tension between the Cereal Killers. Luckily, they put the situation behind them and had since become the best of friends. Even Mona now slept in the group's dormitory instead of her campervan, though Bram still felt she was holding back. This term he was determined to get to know her better so she'd feel comfortable opening up. Maybe it would be a good idea to ask her to go to the Blizzard Bash with him . . .

'Why are you looking at me like that, Bram?' Mona frowned and gripped her magical net, which she used to capture her enemies. It had begun to glow blue. 'Stop being weird.'

Bram took a deep breath to settle the familiar feeling of anxiety in his stomach and decided to summon some of the courage he'd recently found within himself. Being bad *and* confident was hard work. 'Actually, Mona, would you like—?'

The bell ZIIIIIIINNNGGED to announce the end of lunch, cutting off Bram's question. The words died in his throat, and the bravery he'd felt moments before bubbled away. He'd try again later.

He quickly followed his friends out of the food hall and was met by a monstrously chaotic scene in the corridor. Students screamed, pushed, shoved and grabbed each other in their attempt to secure an application form to join the Winter Warts.

Bryan barged towards the noticeboard at the front of the crowd. 'They're all gone!' he roared.

Bram looked around at his fellow students gripping forms to their chests as if their lives depended on it. 'Maybe Felix Frostbite will put out some more,' he said hopefully.

Mona sighed. 'Bram, sometimes in life you need to be in charge of your own destiny and *take* what you want.' She had a devilish glint in her eyes.

Bram smiled wickedly in understanding and took a deep breath, letting his inner villain take over. 'You're right, Mona. There may not be any application forms left on the noticeboard, but there sure are plenty of willing victims who are in possession of a form . . .'

The Cereal Killers grinned back at

him, their plan now solidified.

'Grab and run, gang.

Grab.

And.

Run,'

Bram shouted.

He shot off down the
corridor and pulled application forms out
of as many pupils' hands, paws, jaws and
tentacles as possible, not lingering long
enough to feel their wrath.

Students screamed as Bryan's snapping jaws *ate* their application forms.

Sheila shocked people with her cold body, causing them to get brain freeze.

The Cereal Killers blazed their way through the corridor, leaving everyone in shock, and disappeared out of the other end where they deposited all the forms into Mona's net for safekeeping.

'A genius spurt of evil.' Mona grinned. 'The fewer people that apply, the better chance we all have of getting into the Winter Warts.'

The Cereal Killers cast evil smiles at each other, barely containing their excitement.

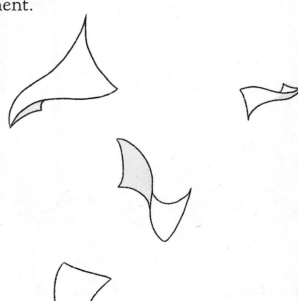

THE
WINTER WARTS

Ever wanted to find a dragon's lair? Watch a dragon
egg hatch? Or learn how to ride one? Come and join
the Winter Warts, the most exclusive club at Villains
Academy, where you'll be taught all there is to know
about dragons by Felix Frostbite and earn extra
de-merits and detentions in the process!

LOCATION: The South Wing

DATE AND TIME: Every Wednesday at sunset

ESSENTIAL EVIL QUALITIES TO JOIN THE WARTS:

☠ A *bad* attitude

☠ At least eight de-merits

☠ Three bars of chocolate (for the dragons)

☠ Sharp talons: optional

☠ NO CAPES!

Application form overleaf. Terms and conditions apply.
Only the best applications from the *evilest* of villains
containing the *baddest* examples of your *wicked*
deeds will be accepted.

Felix Frostbite

Long after the bell had rung to announce the end of lunch, the Cereal Killers rushed into the classroom for their next lesson, having flushed everyone else's Winter Warts application forms down the toilet.

'You're late. Good work,' Felix Frostbite announced as the Cereal Killers sat down. 'Today I want to start with the very basics about ghastly beasts. What do you all know about deadly creatures? Where do you find them? How do you trap them and use them to your advantage?'

Mal's hand shot up impatiently. 'Will we be learning about dragons? My dad once told me a story about his friend who was eaten by one.'

Frostbite shot a spark of frost across the room that froze Mal's fingers

together. 'Don't interrupt me again or
I'll freeze more than just your hand. As
I've said, we're not here to learn about
dragons – only the successful Winter
Warts will have that pleasure. And I'm
sorry to tell you, but your dad's story is
most likely a lie.'

Mal scowled at the teacher. 'No, it's not.'

Mona rolled her eyes. 'Yes, it is. Dragons don't eat people – they're herbivores. They'd only ever eat someone in self-defence. So if your dad's friend really did get eaten, it will be because he's an idiot who wound up a dragon.'

'Oh,' Frostbite said, sarcastically. 'We have a dragon expert in the house, it seems.'

'It's common knowledge,' Mona said, bluntly.

Frostbite frowned. 'Leave the teaching to the *actual* expert. But it's true, dragons are very protective of their nests and children. Before we move on, does anyone know what sort of environment they build their nests in?'

'Caves?' Jeeves the Cat said.

'Wrong.'

'In the clouds?' Sheila said dreamily.

'Wrong again,' Frostbite replied. 'They lay their eggs in trees and suspend them in the branches to stop predators on the ground from eating them. Then the eggs stay in the branches until they're ready to hatch. The special thing about dragon eggs is that they glow. As the dragon grows, the fire inside them becomes brighter. The weak ones fall to the floor because they aren't growing fast or strong enough, whilst the others flourish. That's what makes a dragon's nest so wonderful – you can see it from quite a distance. But a dragon will fiercely defend its eggs, so if you see one, stay clear . . . or be eaten. Lesson one: *always* be aware of your environment. You never know where a ghastly beast may be lurking.'

'Will we get to see a nest?' Sheila asked excitedly. 'Oh, I do love shiny, glowing things! They just dazzle my eyeholes. Apart from you, Bram. I don't like it when you glow because you remind me of a fairy. You almost blinded me when you started glowing in the Mystery Maze. One time, this fairy—'

'Enough,' Frostbite shouted. 'No. You will not see a nest unless you're accepted into the Winter Warts. I'm here to teach you about other ghastly beasts, and that does *not* include dragons. Now I'm going to tell you all about how I became a master of these creatures, and I don't want any more interruptions or questions.'

For the rest of the lesson, the whole of Class Z, apart from Mona, lingered on Felix Frostbite's every word. They listened to how he tracked an army of griffins using only the wind and how he built a shield from long grass to disguise himself from a pack of foulcats. But Bram's mind soon wandered to the Winter Warts application form. If he was going to have any chance of learning about dragons with his friends, he was going to need to embellish his evil achievements. It was time to get creative.

CHAPTER 3

DRAGON THIEF

The rest of the week was filled with endless conversations about Felix Frostbite and the Blizzard Bash. The Cereal Killers filled out their application forms as quickly as they could, making up all sorts of ridiculous accomplishments, and posted them under the teacher's office door in envelopes that tried to bite your fingers off, hoping to score more *evil* points.

Bram's fellow students and the other

teachers were just as starstruck with
Felix Frostbite as Class Z. In Astrology,
Guru Gertrude had predicted that she
would marry him before the end of term,

and in History of Evil, Chief Crabbatus
had asked Frostbite to sign his copy of
The Battles of Badness and then refused
to warm up his fingers after the teacher
had shaken his hand, even when they'd
started turning blue.

But along with Mona, there was one other person who had started to take a dislike to the new teacher . . .

As another day of lessons passed and the sun had almost set, Class Z stood in the Wicked Woods for their final lesson of the week, Physical Escape, and whispered about the unexpected feud brewing between Master Mardybum and Felix Frostbite.

Their form teacher was fed up of being outshone by 'the big-headed, cold oddity named Felix Frostbite' and had been having frequent outbursts. He'd banned the word 'dragon' and any mention of the Winter Warts from his classes, and he seemed moments away from setting up a Frostbite hate club, which Mona was all too happy to join.

Bram thought about how quickly

things had changed within a week. It wasn't long ago that Master Mardybum had been fangirling over Frostbite, and now he couldn't stand the sight of him.

'You need to focus!' Master Mardybum screamed at Class Z. 'Today we will be progressing with our Physical Escape lessons and will be starting to hunt. It's important that you all learn the proper techniques to hunt down your enemies and squash them like slugs. You each have a Villains Academy branded handkerchief, which you must hang out of your back pocket. Apologies in advance for any bogies – I might have used some of them earlier.' The teacher sniggered. 'The aim is to track down each other and steal as many handkerchiefs as you can without getting caught. Think about where your classmates might naturally hide, then look for clues and listen out for noises. The winner of this task will be named Villain of the Week. **HAPPY HUNTING!**' Master Mardybum shot sparks from his fingertips into the sky, signalling the start of the hunt.

Bram made sure his handkerchief was firmly in his back pocket, the tip slightly poking out, and then ran for his life into the woods, the other students dispersing in different directions around him. Sheila shot up into the sky, snatching Jeeves's handkerchief straight out of his pocket. Mr Toad launched himself at Tony and swallowed his handkerchief whole, along

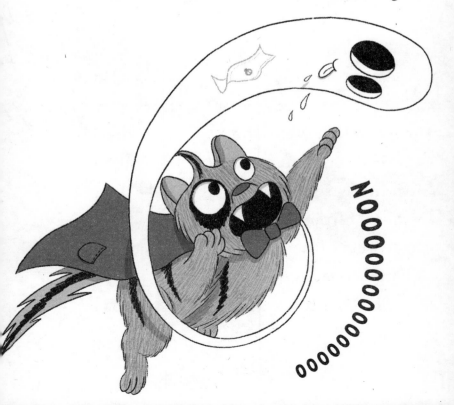

with a finger or two. Bryan lay down for a nap, keeping his handkerchief close, and almost blew Spike the Crocodile away as he let off a deadly fart in his face.

Meanwhile, Mona casually walked through the trees, as if out on a relaxing evening stroll, daring anyone to come near her. Bram followed, hoping to catch her off guard.

'I'd like to see you try to steal from me, Bram,' Mona said out loud, without even turning to look at him. 'Stop lurking behind the trees and come out so I can take your handkerchief from you already.'

'Ha!' Bram replied, as he stepped out from the shadows. 'I'd like to see *you* try to steal from *me*!'

Mona's face split with a wicked smile. 'Challenge accepted.'

She shot towards him as nimble as a

fox, swiping at him with her net. Bram
screamed, equally terrified and excited,
and ran like the wind. He jumped over
roots, rolled under fallen trees and
dashed through undergrowth to get
away from Mona, ending up well outside
the boundary that Master Mardybum
had set.

'I'm an expert huntress, Bram,'
Mona jeered as she caught up with
him, stretching out towards his back
pocket. Her hand
clasped on to
the handkerchief
like a vice and
before
Bram
could do
anything
to stop

her, it was stolen from him.

'That was fun,' Mona said, chuckling. 'You put up a good fight.'

'Thanks.' Bram smiled before realizing how quickly night had fallen since the start of the lesson.

Looking around the clearing they were in, Bram noticed that some of the trees were shining with balls of light that shimmered like a kaleidoscope.

'How far have we come?' Bram said,

 his eyes wide with wonder as he took in the beauty of the Wicked Woods. 'We should probably get back to the rest of the class.'

'Wait!' Mona said in warning as her eyes darted between the trees. 'Don't move.'

Bram's body stiffened with panic. 'What is it? If this is one of your tricks—'

'I'm not joking around,' Mona stated. 'We need to get out of here as quickly and quietly as possible. Don't make any sudden movements or loud noises.'

'Why?' Bram's voice wobbled.

'Because we're standing in the middle of a dragon's nest,' Mona said calmly.

Bram tried not to descend into full-blown panic. How could Mona not be terrified right now? How was she so calm and collected? Surely she was just as frightened as he was?

Bram opened his mouth to scream, but Mona slapped one of her hands across it and placed her finger over her lips for him to stay quiet. 'A dragon will only eat you to defend its nest,' Mona whispered. 'If we leave now without alerting it, we'll be fine. Compose yourself and stay calm!'

Bram nodded and took Mona's lead. They lowered themselves to the ground so they were less noticeable, and crawled away from the dragon's nest as quickly as they could. Mona moved swiftly ahead, but Bram suddenly came to a stop as his attention was caught by a small dragon egg on the floor in front of him. Its surface flickered with a faint glow and a thin crack ran along the length of the shell.

'The weak ones fall to the floor,' Felix Frostbite had said, and Bram's heart dropped at the realization. He couldn't leave this baby dragon to die. When he joined Villains Academy, he had been the weak one. He still was, in some respects. But everyone deserved a chance to beat the odds and prove themselves, like Bram had in the Mystery Maze.

In a split second, he made a decision, thrusting the egg into his pocket and hurrying after Mona. He'd return it later when it was strong enough to survive on its own.

'Come on, slowpoke,' Mona whispered

with an annoyed glance back towards
Bram. 'What's taking you so long?'

'Nothing,' Bram muttered as he
followed her out of the clearing.

In the distance, Master Mardybum
shot sparks of fire into the sky to signal
the end of the lesson.

'Thank the devil,' Bram sighed in
relief. 'Physical Escape is the *worst*.'

Mona nodded and walked beside
Bram in silence. He attempted to make
conversation with her, hoping to get her
to open up about their terrifying ordeal,
but she gave nothing away, her hard
exterior remaining impenetrable.

Bram's mind drifted back to the dragon egg in his pocket and he wondered what he was going to do with it. Did he really have the time or resources to look after it? Where was he going to keep it? What would he tell the others? He hadn't thought this through at all, but it was too late to go back now.

Bram and Mona joined the rest of Class Z who were now all gathered next to Master Mardybum.

'I hope you had a villainously bad time,' the teacher said. 'Now for the important part. Let's find out who the winner is!' He went around the class, taking handkerchiefs from the students and counting who had stolen the most. Bram dipped his head and avoided eye contact as Master Mardybum passed by, smirking at his lack of handkerchiefs. Mona handed hers over quickly and glanced at the floor, which Bram thought was unusual given how much she usually gloated.

'Well, it appears that some of you did *very* well in this challenge. Others, not so much . . .' Master Mardybum said. 'I'm pleased to announce that the winner of the hunt, and this week's Villain of the Week is . . . Mr Toad! Congratulations.

Now, if you wouldn't mind dry-cleaning
the handkerchiefs and returning them to
my office once you've regurgitated them,
that would be marvellous.'

Mr Toad burped with joy, and the class
walked back towards Villains Academy
for dinner.

Mona turned to the Cereal Killers
as they reached the entrance. 'I'm
feeling really tired all of a sudden, so
I'm going to skip dinner tonight. I'll see

you tomorrow,' she said before quickly walking away.

'Is she all right?' Bryan asked with a frown.

'I don't know. She's been quiet and off with me since the end of the hunt,' Bram replied, feeling confused.

As they sat down in the food hall to eat, Bram couldn't help but worry. Had he done something to upset Mona? Did she blame him for leading them to a dragon's nest? What if she didn't want to spend time with him any more? After a few mouthfuls of silly con carne, which Cook shaped into terrifying faces on their plates, Bram's appetite had

BYEEEEEE

completely disappeared and he pushed the remaining food around, wanting nothing more than to climb into bed.

'I'm going to head up. I'm not feeling that hungry,' Bram said to his friends.

'Bagsy having your dessert!' Sheila screeched.

Bram smiled. 'Goodnight, gang. Dream bad.'

As he walked up the stairs to their dormitory, his hand settled on the dragon egg in his pocket. He needed to come up with a plan, and fast.

CHAPTER 4

BUBBLE AND TROUBLE

Bram woke to the loud noise of the
Cereal Killers getting ready for the day.
When he'd got back to the dormitory
last night, Mona was already tucked up
in bed fast asleep, the room shrouded in
darkness. Careful not to wake her, Bram
had crept over to his chest of drawers
and temporarily hidden the dragon egg
amongst his underwear. The egg was
slightly too big for him to be able to close

the drawer entirely, but it was enough
to keep it out of sight of prying eyes.
Now, after a restless sleep, he yawned
and rolled out of bed, immediately
thinking about the egg.

'READY FOR A BIG, BAD DAY!'

Sheila yelled her usual morning greeting.

PLEASE
STOP.

Bryan groaned. 'Sheila, we've had this conversation *so* many times. You need to be quiet until at least ten in the morning on weekends.'

'Oh, shush, sonny peep. You're such a grumpy mare.'

Bram strolled over to his underwear drawer, wary of attracting attention, and pulled it open quietly.

His heart stopped. The egg was nowhere to be seen.

As he rifled through his pants, throwing them out of the drawer and around the room, panic flooded his entire body. One pair flew through Sheila's head, who screamed in delight, another soared into Tony's eye socket, and Mona caught a few in her net.

Bram removed the last pair of pants and then whipped round to face his friends. 'Has someone been in my underwear drawer?!' he asked.

'*No*. What are you implying, Bram? Why would I go anywhere near your underwear drawer . . . ?' Sheila snapped back hurriedly.

'I didn't say *you*, I asked if *someone* had, but you're acting very suspicious, Sheila.' Bram frowned.

'Fine!' Sheila said. 'But it's not my fault you left it open, and it really annoyed me. Learn to close your drawers properly in future, sonny peep.'

Bram stormed towards her. 'Well, you shouldn't have looked inside. There are private things in there . . .' He trailed off, stopping himself from spilling his secret.

'What private things?' Bryan asked with a yawn.

Mona narrowed her eyes at Bram suspiciously.

'Yeah, what are you missing?' Sheila smirked.

Bram didn't rise to the bait. He knew that Sheila had taken his dragon egg and he was worried about what she was going to do with the information.

In the corner of the room, Mona began searching through her own underwear drawer, fear etched on her face.

'Someone's been in my drawer too.'

'You're both very unimaginative.'
Sheila grinned. 'Underwear drawers
are the most common hiding place, so
it's always the first location I look for
secrets, *especially* if they're left open.'

Tony screwed his head on, ready for
the day. 'What secrets?'

'Thief!' Mona yelled. 'Give it back
now, Sheila. It's not yours.'

Sheila giggled and twirled around the
room. 'What deliciously yummy eggs
they were!'

'NO!' Bram and Mona bellowed in
unison. Bram jumped on to the bed,
trying to catch the ghost, whilst Mona
lunged at her with her net.

'Ha! You should see your faces, sonny
peeps!' Sheila laughed, staying well out
of reach. 'Of course I didn't eat them. I'm

not a monster! I know dragon eggs when I see them.'

'DRAGON EGGS?'

Tony shouted.

'*Wow*, real dragon eggs? Where did you find them?' Bryan whispered in disbelief. 'Can I see them?'

Bram stared at Mona. Mona stared at Bram. So she'd stolen a dragon egg too. Was that why she'd been acting so strange last night?

'Fine. You caught us,' Mona said bluntly. 'Bram and I accidentally stumbled upon a dragon's nest yesterday during Physical Escape, and I happened to come across a rogue egg on the floor that needed help . . . so I took it. It appears Bram found himself in the same situation. So, if you don't mind, Sheila, we'd like them back.'

'There's a slight problem with that . . .' Sheila trailed off.

'*What*?' Bram and Mona both groaned together.

'I can't remember where I put them . . .'

'Nope, not in here,' Bram shouted as he edged out of one of the cleaning mice's tunnels, being extra careful *not* to get his bum stuck like the time he'd tried to break into detention in Master Mardybum's office.

'Sheila, remind us again exactly where you went last night,' Mona said with her arms crossed.

'I couldn't sleep, so I went to the kitchen for a snack. Then I got caught and chased by Cook, which was very fun! Then I went for a long walk around the halls before going back to the dormitory. Oh, I might have had a bath too.'

'Ugh, so you went everywhere,' Bryan said grumpily, his belly gurgling loudly from lack of food. 'I still don't see why we couldn't have had breakfast *before* searching for the eggs. It's not like we have any classes at the weekend.'

'You're such a hangry soul sometimes, fluffpot,' Sheila said, stroking his mane. Bryan attempted to bite her tail.

'I'm with Bryan on this one,' Tony agreed. 'My bones are withering away here!'

Despite the complaints, the Cereal Killers continued searching high and low for the missing dragon eggs, getting hangrier by the minute. There were no eggs in the kitchen and Cook threatened to make them into a stew if she ever saw them near her kitchen again. There were none in the classrooms, the library or any

of the corridors. The figures in the picture frames that decorated the halls and stairs of the school refused to help, and one even tried to *bite* Bram's

paw off when he politely asked for help. Their final destination was the bathroom and as they hurried through the door to begin searching there was a loud

CRACKLE.

'What was that?' Mona said, her eyes wide with suspicion.

FIZZ.

'Are you farting, Bryan?' Sheila asked.

'No, I'm not,' said Bryan, defending himself. 'I think the sound is coming from the tub.'

In the middle of the room, the huge swimming-pool-sized bathtub oozed with foam and water. Bram squinted at the suds. He was certain his eyes were deceiving him, but it looked like the bubbles were shimmering with iridescent light. Just as he was about to move on, the most incredible sight revealed itself within the foam.

Two dazzling dragon eggs.

Their insides swirled with magic, and the crackling and fizzing grew louder as the light became more dazzling.

The water suddenly began to spit, and bubbles and foam burst out of the bath. Bram realized they were seconds away from watching the dragons hatch.

The gang dropped to the floor and covered their heads as an ear-splitting *POP* exploded through the air and two baby dragons were born in the bathtub.

'The bathwater must have emulated their mother's warmth and made them hatch,' Mona said, wiping bubbles off her face.

'Crikey!' Tony bellowed, his jaw on the floor in shock. 'What a palaver we're in now.'

Screeches of delight echoed around the room and glimmering bubbles floated through the air as the dragons thrashed in the water. One of them had vibrant emerald and sea-blue feathered scales with pearl-like eyes. Two small teeth stuck out from an underbite, and tiny tendrils of smoke drifted from its nostrils. The other one had scales that were a golden sunset orange, and its whole body, particularly its delicate wings, was much larger than its sibling's.

'WHAT FUN!' Sheila shouted and

jumped into the large bath with the dragons. They chased after her and snapped their jaws with joy.

'Don't just stand there!' Mona screeched. 'CATCH THEM!'

The Cereal Killers darted around the bath after the dragons. Bryan splashed and leapt through the water in an attempt to grab them. Tony made bubble beards, trying to distract and entertain them so

someone else could snatch them, but it only made them more excited. Sheila unhelpfully squealed in delight and jumped out of the froth to scare everyone. Bram ran around, trying to catch them, but they hopped out of his grasp every time he got near. And Mona swung her net frantically, charging the bubbles with electrifying light that illuminated the room with a rainbow glow.

'AHHHHHHHH!' Sheila screamed as the dragons bit and licked her tail. 'IT TICKLES! STOP! Can you taste the cake from my kitchen visit last night? I did get covered in chocolate frosting as Cook—'

In a swift swoop, whilst the dragons were distracted by Sheila's chocolate-covered tail, Mona scooped them up in her net. They wriggled and wrestled against the ropes, but the thing about Mona's net was that once you were in, there was no way of getting out without her say-so.

The Cereal Killers cheered around her, soaked from head to toe with foamy bubbles.

'Now what?' Tony said in realization. 'What are we going to do with two baby dragons? And how are we going to get them out of here without anyone seeing us? The teachers will sever our limbs if we're caught. My limbs are all I have!'

'I think severed limbs are the least of our problems,' Bram replied, staring at the baby dragons. His mind was in overdrive thinking about the amount of trouble he and Mona had caused. But he wasn't going to let his friends see him crumble. *He* was going to be the one to fix this. 'C'mon, gang. I think I have a plan.'

CHAPTER 5

BRAIN FREEZE

The friends stashed the baby dragons in Mona's old campervan, now dubbed the Cereal Killers' campervan. They deposited them down the laundry chute in the bathroom to avoid being caught, and then smuggled them across the grounds to the van with the intention of setting them free in the Wicked Woods once everyone had gone to bed that night.

But when night fell, the Cereal Killers

realized they weren't ready to say goodbye to their new pets. And as the weekend drew to a close, the gang planned to take shifts skiving lessons so they could continue looking after the dragons. Though skiving was easier said than done, and their excuses got wilder by the minute.

Sheila said that she was tending to her laundry; Tony explained that he had been searching the graves in the grounds of Villains Academy for a new hip; Bryan stated he was allergic to learning. Bram lied multiple times about oversleeping and once over-explained that he had got into a fight with the cleaner mice over a rogue sock. Mona was the only one who kept her cool and didn't justify her lack of attendance. In fact, she said she'd destroy anyone who dared to ask, which thoroughly impressed most of her teachers, apart from Felix Frostbite, who had taken a dislike to her for her sullen attitude towards him.

As the weeks wore on, Bram stopped enjoying skipping lessons to look after the baby dragons. They nipped at his toes and had the foulest-smelling breath. And they ate a *lot*. In just over two weeks, they'd trebled in size, and Bram didn't know how much longer the Cereal Killers would be able to hide their secret in the campervan. Whilst stealing the egg had seemed like a good idea at the time to protect a vulnerable dragon and simultaneously prove his badness, Bram was regretting it. They were in too deep.

One evening whilst Bram was skiving

Astrology, the smaller dragon, now
named Alfonso, chased Bram around
for three hours straight, licking his fur
until he smelt like a manky cabbage. The

larger, orange dragon, now named Jaxon,
constantly whined for more food, but as
there was only so much the group could
smuggle out at mealtimes, Bram resorted
to feeding them from his personal supply

of chocolate to keep them quiet, even though it only seemed to give them more energy.

Mona, on the other hand, reported no news from her shifts with the dragons and said they were as good as gold. One time, Bram snuck out to check on her during her shift to see if she was lying, and to his disappointment, she was right. Both dragons lay napping beside her, until Bram's lurking movements outside startled them, causing Jaxon to let out a big fiery breath that nearly removed Bram's eyebrows. Mona said it served him right for snooping.

At the same time, talk of the Blizzard Bash had intensified as posters appeared in the corridors of the school, and mealtimes were filled with students awkwardly asking each other to the

ball. Mona went deathly quiet every time it was mentioned and threatened to use her net on anyone who broached the subject with her. Bram still had nobody to go with and had even considered not attending, but he didn't want to miss out on all the fun. Plus, he'd been practising alone, and his dancing was getting quite good!

The acceptance list for the Winter Warts had also finally been released after Felix Frostbite had spent weeks deliberating who would be worthy of a place. To nobody's surprise (because they'd stolen all the application forms) the Cereal Killers had been accepted, along with three of their

rivals from the Overlords
– Mal, the Tooth Hairy
and Mr Toad. Seven
other lucky students
from different classes
and year groups brought
the total to fifteen.

- Vampy
- Sarah
- Mal
- The Tooth Hairy
- Mr Toad
- Raven
- Bram
- Mona
- Bryan
- Tony
- Sheila
- Lois
- Gary
- Salt
- Pepper

Tonight was the first
official meeting of the
Winter Warts, and the
Cereal Killers walked
through the halls towards
Felix Frostbite's office in the South Wing.
Bryan had brushed his mane for the
evening and Tony had even flossed his
eyeholes.

'Are you sure we shouldn't tell
Frostbite about the dragons?' Sheila
said with a sigh. She'd just come from a
particularly tiring shift where the two

dragons had almost set the campervan on fire. 'He could help us, and it might even impress him!'

'No way,' Mona snapped. 'We're not telling *anyone*, especially not Frostbite. If the dragons' parents find out that we took them, they'll decide to stop defending Villains Academy and leave us open to attack. I want to graduate Villains Academy and be a famous villain, not ruin the future of the school.'

'He could find a way for us to avoid that, though,' Bram replied.

'No!' Mona yelled. 'We don't know him, so we can't trust him. Real villains don't trust people easily, Bram.'

Bram flinched at Mona's outburst. Was that why she had a hard time trusting the Cereal Killers?

'My, my. Fighting already, are we? I'm impressed.' Felix Frostbite stood in the doorway of his office, grinning down at the Cereal Killers. 'Come in. You're the last to arrive.'

'*That's because you took so long with your hair,*' Tony whispered to Bryan.

LOOKING FABULOUS, THOUGH.

Felix Frostbite's office was three times the size of Master Mardybum's. The walls and ceiling were covered in a thin layer of frost, making the whole room twinkle like a diamond and crackle as new ice formed. A cold mist ran along the floorboards, sharp spikes of ice jutted out from the furniture and dragon ice sculptures towered into the air. In the middle of the room there was a round seating area made from a gigantic dragon's egg, and in the centre of it a blue fire flickered and roared as if a dragon's fiery breath was keeping it alight.

Bram pulled the sleeves of his jumper down. The room was beautiful but *freezing*, and he wasn't the only one who thought so. In the dragon-egg seating area, a gargoyle sat frozen with icicles

dripping from its nose, a raven with a
monocle shivered violently, a pair of
terrifying twins scowled, and a vampire
gnome, ghost girl and humongous hairy
spider huddled close to keep warm.
Mal, the Tooth Hairy and Mr Toad
all frowned at the Cereal Killers with
disgust as they took their places.

'Welcome, Warts,' Frostbite began.
'Now you might be wondering what

exactly happens when you become a Wart. Well, I'm happy to reveal that this isn't just any old club. No, the reason why I've gathered this select group is because I believe all of you have what it takes to become the new generation of dragon riders. And who better to teach you than the most infamous dragon rider of them all: me!'

Gasps echoed around the room, whilst

Tony's jaw chattered loudly. Bram sat on the edge of his seat and wondered whether it would be cool or not to make notes.

'However, even after training, some of you might not be able to ride a dragon, as they only accept the *baddest* villains on their back. But I hope that I can steer you all in the right direction . . .' Frostbite trailed off, admiring his own reflection in an ice sculpture. 'So, in today's meeting, I'll be teaching you how to befriend a dragon. Though do not mistake my wording – dragons are *not* and will never be your friends. You should see them more as acquaintances or allies. Dragons are free spirits, but if you know how, you can work with them and even *control* them.' A wicked grin appeared on Frostbite's face.

'It's very c-c-c-cold,' Tony whispered to his friends, his jaw chattering uncontrollably.

Sheila shushed him and frowned, but Bram nodded in sympathy, rubbing his paws together. They had began to gather frost.

Frostbite continued, 'You can hunt a dragon down if you know what signs to look for. They like the dark and the cold so can usually be found in forests, caves, or the depths of the earth. If you find one, make sure you have chocolate on you. Dragons *love* chocolate. It makes them sleepy and *slightly* more friendly.'

Bram grinned as Frostbite relayed this information because he'd already found out that Alfonso and Jaxon liked chocolate, although it hadn't seemed to make them sleepy.

'Right, come on. Up you get, you lazy bones,' Frostbite encouraged. 'Let's work on your auras. Dragons can sense fear, so when you approach them, you need to learn to hide it from them. Place your feet firmly on the floor and adopt a strong stance. Then clench your jaw and try not to let your body tremble. That might be easier for some of you than others.'

Tony had begun to shake up and down from the cold, his jaw rattling like a chainsaw.

'B-B-B-BRAIN-F-F-F-FREEZE!'

he screeched.

'Fight it, Tony!'
Frostbite commanded.

The teacher stood in front of Tony
with a ferocious expression on his face
that would rival an angry dragon, his
eyes burning Arctic blue. But if Tony was
scared, he didn't show it. His bones jiggled
and jittered so violently that he started
vibrating in a circle around the room,
unable to control his own body. His left
foot flew across the office, almost taking
out Mr Toad and the spider. Wild noises

escaped his mouth and he screamed
'**B-B-B-BRAIN-F-F-F-FREEZE!**' on
a loop. The other students found it
hilarious, and Mal clapped in glee. Sheila
joined in with Tony, hopping around like
a fool as if practising her dance moves for
the Blizzard Bash.

'Stop this nonsense!' Frostbite roared.

But whilst everyone tried to listen to the
dragon master, nobody could concentrate
when Tony's bones were flying everywhere.
Students dodged flailing limbs. Mona
caught rogue fingers in her net. Bram
hopped from foot to foot, trying not to
stand on the frozen floorboards for too
long. And Bryan clumsily bounded around
the room trying to catch Tony, but as he
turned a corner, his body bashed into one
of the ginormous dragon ice sculptures,
sending it soaring.

As if in slow motion, the dragon head smashed into Frostbite's desk and sent his paperwork flying into the air like confetti. The room fell completely silent, and seconds later the teacher descended on the class in fury.

OOPS

Everyone suddenly began cleaning up the mess to avoid Frostbite's wrath. Bram rushed to pick up the spilt papers, grabbing sheet upon sheet of teacher notes, report cards and a map of the school that had been annotated. In the corner of the map, the Wicked Woods had been furiously circled with a note that said 'HERE BE DRAGONS!' along with scribbles that read 'MINE', 'ATTACK' and 'DESTROY'.

Bram stopped, frozen. It looked like a plan. A plan to steal something . . .

His heart began to beat fast as the words swirled around in his brain. But he wiped his sweaty palms on his trousers and placed the crumpled paperwork back on Frostbite's desk as if he hadn't seen a thing.

It was harmless and normal for Frostbite to be looking for dragons, wasn't it? He was a dragon master after all. But Mona's warnings about Frostbite swam up to the surface and doubts crept into Bram's mind.

As Bram sat back down in the seating area and attempted to settle his nerves, Frostbite continued the Winter Warts' first lesson. But the atmosphere in the room had turned frosty and the dragon master's eyes bore into Bram's soul and glimmered with threat.

Felix Frostbite knew that Bram had seen his plans. *Gulp*.

CHAPTER 6

A BREWING DISASTER

Word of the commotion at the Winter Warts meeting spread around the school like wildfire. Rumours transformed into much bigger lies, and the latest story circulating was that one of the giant dragon ice sculptures had come to life and almost eaten everyone in the entire club.

As Class Z waited in the greenhouse for Poisons the following day, Bram told the Cereal Killers about the suspicious plans he'd seen in Felix Frostbite's office. He'd kept it to himself last night, wondering whether he was overreacting, but worry had been consuming him all day, and he couldn't hold it in any longer.

'Don't be so silly.' Bryan yawned. 'The cold must have got to your head yesterday.'

'Brain freeze is no laughing matter, I'll have you know,' Tony replied. 'But I agree, Frostbite wouldn't steal the dragons away from the school. You must have got yourself confused, Bram.'

'Yeah, stop being so dramatic,' Sheila added.

'I'm not,' Bram defended himself. 'What do you think, Mona?' He turned to his friend, who had remained strangely quiet throughout the conversation.

'I told you so.' Mona frowned. 'I've

said all along that I had a bad feeling about him, and now you've proved me right.'

'Oh, *whatever*,' Sheila wailed. 'Looks like there's a second member of the Frostbite hate club now.'

'Ignore her.' Mona turned to Bram.

'But what if he actually *is* trying to steal the dragons?' Bram asked.

Mona shook her head and lowered her voice. 'Don't worry about that right now. Let's start by trying to gather evidence that he's up to no good. But don't mention this to anyone else – we don't want Frostbite to know we're on to him. We need to catch him off guard. Okay?'

Bram nodded reluctantly as Master Mardybum swished into the greenhouse.

'Today we will be brewing a senseless poison, which confuses a victim's vision,

hearing and sense of smell,' Master Mardybum began. 'It was most famously used in the Clash of Chaos when evil mastermind Captain Chaos covered the city of Dreadmount with a cloud of it. This caused everyone to lose control of their senses and ultimately allowed him to defeat the civilians as easily as squishing an ant. It's a fabulous poison to use against your enemies, but it's extremely difficult to brew, so it's essential that you LISTEN,' Master Mardybum roared at the Overlords, who were busy chatting amongst themselves. 'Get it wrong and it will blow up like a constipated sprout. Today you will be working in your teams to brew the poison following the method on the board. Please, and I beg you, don't bother me unless completely necessary,' the teacher finished as he lounged back in his chair for a nap, complete with flowery eye mask.

The Cereal Killers immediately looked to Mona for instructions. She was the *best* at brewing poison.

'Sir,' Mal bravely began, 'is it true that poison doesn't work on dragons?'

Master Mardybum sighed and lounged deeper into his chair. Without removing the eye mask, he said, 'Yes and no. You'd need a *lot* of poison to take down a dragon and it would have to be super strong. They can withstand most poisons, though chocolate does make them rather sleepy. I daresay they could probably withstand Bryan's farts too. Now don't mention dragons or any other irritating buzzwords again. Unless you want me to brew you into a poison . . .'

Mona looked at the Cereal Killers. 'Are you going to help me with this poison, or are you all going to stand there like lemons?'

'Your servants are here to be of service.' Sheila saluted. 'What can we do for you?'

'Sheila, I need you to mix the fringlefang juice until it's frothy. Not a

YES, MA'AM!

paste. Frothy. Don't overmix it,' Mona
said. 'Bryan, you can pummel the sorrel
stones into a mush. Tony, can you go and
find some wragweed? It grows on that
plant in the corner with the red leaves.
We need a big handful. Bram, you can
help me with this nightshade.'

The friends did as they were told.
Nobody messed with Mona when she
was making poison because they were
afraid she'd poison them at mealtimes as
payback.

'What do you need me to do?' Bram asked, looking at a pile of jet-black berries.

'We need to carefully peel off the skins of these nightshade berries. The skin is rich in nutrients and will help develop the potency of the poison,' Mona replied happily.

'Okay,' Bram responded and slowly began slicing the skin off the berries. This was the first moment he'd had alone with Mona all week, so he decided to take the opportunity to try to get her to open up to him. 'Have you always loved making poison?'

'Yes,' Mona said. 'And be careful not to cut the berries too deep. They'll explode if you do . . . and they'll stain your skin purple for weeks.'

'Noted,' Bram grimaced. 'Where did you learn about all of this?'

'My parents are really talented poison makers,' Mona replied with a sad smile. 'I didn't get to see my mum or dad that much growing up. They were always too busy being evil villains and destroying the world. But when they *were* around, we made poison together. I always tried so hard to impress them, but I don't think I ever managed to. They're much better villains than I'll ever be.' Mona tipped her head down so the brim of her hat covered her face. Her feet shuffled on the floor, and she awkwardly twiddled her thumbs.

Bram thought about how difficult it must have been for Mona to live in her parents' shadow. No wonder she cared so much about her performance at Villains Academy and didn't let friendships distract her.

'I know how you feel,' he said. 'My dads are super bad and I'm desperate to prove to them, and everyone else, that I'm bad too. That's one of the reasons I stole the dragon egg.'

Mona shuffled closer to Bram, their elbows brushing against each other. 'Me too. I wanted to prove that I'm bad enough to ride a dragon. I reckon we'll be

able to ride one when we've finished the Winter Warts training,' Mona said with a smile, before lowering her voice. 'Unless a certain someone destroys us all first.'

'He'll never get past us,' Bram said with a smirk. 'He'll have a fight on his hands if the Cereal Killers have anything to do with it!'

'Well, two of the Cereal Killers. But I'm not sure I'd trust Sheila on a dragon anyway.' Mona chuckled.

'Me neither.' Bram laughed. 'We're not so different, though. We're all just desperate to prove how bad we are. I'm glad we've got each other.'

'Me too. Now stop being so disgustingly nice or I'll have to hurt you,' Mona said with a straight face. 'Though I'm proud that you haven't let Frostbite's fame distract you and stop you from seeing the truth about him. Maybe you are becoming a true villain after all.'

'Thank you,' Bram mumbled. 'So what are we going to do about him?'

Mona grinned. 'We're going to take him down. Let's dig for more dirt and try to get him sacked. He won't be able to steal anything from the school if he doesn't work here.'

'Okay.' Bram smiled and reached into his pocket. 'Want some chocolate to celebrate our evil scheme?'

'Chocolate?' Mona asked, confused.

'Yeah,' Bram said. 'I carry it everywhere with me now because the dragons in the campervan *love* it. I had such a peaceful shift the other night. They didn't bite me once! Most of us keep it on us. Not that you need it, of course. You seem to have a special way with them. Though Sheila tends to eat her chocolate supply straight away and then badgers everyone else for theirs.'

Mona's eyes grew wide.

'What?' Bram asked, alarmed. 'Have I got something on my face?'

'Oh, *no*,' she whispered and batted the chocolate out of Bram's hand, sending it flying through the greenhouse.

BANG!

The room exploded with a shocking flash of green, and the air filled with the putrid smell of burning sprouts.

'What in the name of the devil is going on?' Master Mardybum shouted as he woke from his slumber in fright.

'Fringlefang juice reacts with chocolate,' Mona said to Bram bluntly.

Out of the acrid dust, a burnt-looking Sheila, Tony and Bryan emerged with their faces covered in black soot.

'Who farted?' Sheila said with a frown. 'It stinks in here.'

Master Mardybum scowled at the Cereal Killers. 'I expected better from

your team. If you don't pass your exam at the end of term, none of you will be attending the Blizzard Bash. Now clean up this mess whilst I go back to sleep.'

The friends reluctantly began clearing up. Tony and Bryan swept up the debris, whilst Sheila busied herself by drawing a moustache in the black soot. Bram picked up the ingredients that had gone flying from the workstation and noticed Mona pocketing a vial of fringlefang juice as she tidied up. He wondered what type of poison she'd be making outside of class.

By the time the lesson was over, the Cereal Killers had managed to produce a perfect senseless poison, much to the delight of Master Mardybum, who said, 'Maybe you aren't such senseless nitwits after all.'

CHAPTER 7

GURU GERTRUDE'S WARNING

Nerves grew at Villains Academy as the end-of-term exam and the Blizzard Bash loomed closer. The teachers relished teasing the students and forced mock exams upon them whenever they felt like it.

Matron Bones, the teacher of Deadly Injuries, threw bones at students' heads and had them guess what species they came from. If they identified the bone wrongly, she whacked them over the head with it until the information stayed in their brain, which led to most of the pupils leaving her class with banging headaches.

The following week, Professor Pluto, the teacher of Bad Language, screamed profanities in Class Z's eardrums and explained if the insult wasn't loud, then it wasn't worth giving. So when Bram dared to mumble his homework, a poem he'd written about being bad, she wrote SHUBBLEMEGUMP (a terrible insult that nobody knew the meaning of) across his forehead and said that one day the words would sink in.

Whiz Warmbottom, the teacher of Villainous Qualities, muttered under his breath that nobody had magical qualities bad enough to be a villain, and when he tried to coax a magical skill out of Bryan, a deadly fart escaped instead.

Master Mardybum had become extremely strict every time anyone messed up a poison or got caught in Physical Escape. And rumour had it that he'd stuck up a photo of Felix Frostbite in his store cupboard and screamed at it when he needed to let out his anger.

In the Winter Warts meetings, Felix Frostbite kept them busy by teaching everyone the correct way to mount a dragon and how to grip and balance on one when aboard. However, the teacher had become increasingly cold towards the Cereal Killers, in particular Bram and Mona. Bram suspected it was because he knew they were on to him. Mona attempted many times to prise information out of Frostbite, but his replies were always vague and blunt, only drawing more suspicion his way.

Today they were practising how to climb on to a life-size model of a dragon made from ice, which was as difficult as it sounded. Bram slipped and slid all over it. Bryan gave up and said it wasn't worth the hassle. Tony's head fell off as he threw himself into it. Mal, the Tooth Hairy and Mr Toad mounted successfully . . . but after climbing on each other's shoulders. Mona was the only one who ascended gracefully without any trouble.

'Now what?' she said with a cocky smirk in Frostbite's direction. 'Do I fly it and *steal* away into the night?'

Bram's shoulders tensed. He knew what Mona was doing. She was trying to trip up their teacher so he'd reveal his plans. But her brashness only made Bram worry.

Frostbite glared at Mona, his eyes twinkling with menace. 'It would probably throw you right off.'

'We'll see,' Mona said as she slid off the ice sculpture. 'Dragons tend to like me.'

Then she walked away without another word.

Bram glanced at Mona then back at Frostbite. Had she just revealed too much about their campervan secret?

The dragons continued to get bigger by the day, and as one week rolled into the next, they started to outgrow

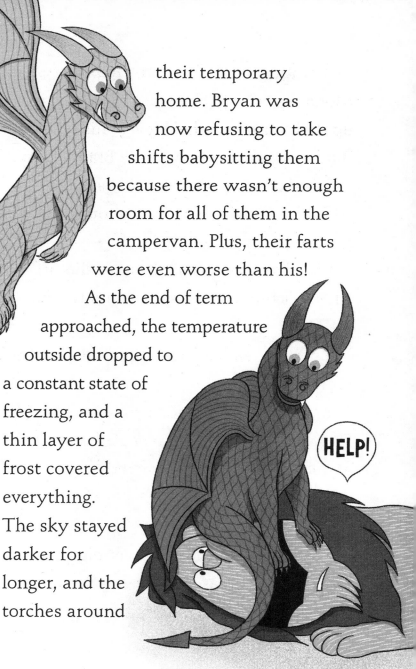

their temporary home. Bryan was now refusing to take shifts babysitting them because there wasn't enough room for all of them in the campervan. Plus, their farts were even worse than his!

As the end of term approached, the temperature outside dropped to a constant state of freezing, and a thin layer of frost covered everything. The sky stayed darker for longer, and the torches around

HELP!

Villains Academy were constantly lit for light and heat. Cosy season was well and truly upon them, and Bram relished the warmth of the knitted jumpers that one of his dads had made him from the wool of terrified sheep. He would be going home to them for the holidays, and he couldn't wait to tell them all about his adventures.

As the final week of term began, and the dreaded exam was now almost upon them, Class Z sat on the lawn outside Villains Academy with their necks craned up to the sky, pretending to be

in store for them.

'I see a dazzling glitterball, sparkling outfits, a spectacular performance from a band long dead, and a *kiss*! Yes, a kiss, with my beloved Felix Frostbite,' Guru Gertrude shouted.

'I could have predicted that, although the kiss seems far-fetched. Thank the devil this class is almost over,' Mona complained.

'I see a wedding,' Sheila said confidently, her body shimmering as the moonlight shone down on her.

Guru Gertrude's eyes bulged out of her head. 'A wedding?' she whispered. 'Go on, my villain. What else do you see?'

The Cereal Killers held in their laughter as Sheila continued. 'A white dress. A massive celebration. A CAKE!'

'Oh, my devils, you truly have the sight! What a wonderful gift,' Guru Gertrude exclaimed and enveloped Sheila in a hug. She swiftly moved on to bother the scowling Overlords, and began to ask if any of them had seen her glorious wedding too.

'And that, my friends, is how you pass Guru Gertrude's class. Tell her what she wants to hear.' Sheila beamed.

'Sheila, that was mean!' Bram replied with a smirk. He secretly admired Sheila's tactic of lying to get on their teacher's *bad* side.

'Truly evil,' Mona said with a grin.

The Overlords didn't play to Guru Gertrude's desires, which let her bereft and irritable for the remainder of the lesson. She continued to teach them about reading the stars to predict the future, but by this point everyone had switched off and was tired of her nonsense.

As the bell rang to mark the end of the day, Guru Gertrude stiffened.

'DEATH!'

she shouted as her body began to shake.

'DEATH OF
VILLAINS
ACADEMY!

DEATH OF THE DRAGONS!

A THIEF IN THE NIGHT!

DARKNESS FOR ALL!

Oh, and don't forget your exam at nine
a.m. tomorrow in the library.'

Class Z looked at each other in bewilderment, some holding in laughter, but Bram's heart had started to pound. Given what he knew about Felix Frostbite, Guru Gertrude's predictions rang true.

'What rubbish,' Mr Toad chirped.

Tony agreed and began walking away. The Cereal Killers followed him across the grounds of Villains Academy towards their campervan to check on the dragons before dinner.

'Do you think Guru Gertrude's predictions are right?' Bram asked. 'Death of Villains Academy and the dragons? It does align with the plans I saw in Frostbite's office.'

'Oh, Bram, will you let it go, funshine?' Sheila replied. 'None of her predictions ever come true. You don't *really* think she's going to kiss Frostbite, do you?'

'Maybe.' Bram shrugged.

'Oh, stop being so naïve.' Bryan frowned. 'You just want to be proved right that Frostbite is up to something when he's not. He's a world-renowned villain after all.'

'He *is* up to something!' Bram said defensively. 'You're all too blinded by his fame.'

'Okay, let's not argue,' Mona jumped in. 'We all need to remain calm or we'll rile up the dragons.'

'Do you want to shout that any louder?' Bram whispered furiously. 'Just announce it to the whole of Villains Academy, why don't you?'

'Oh, nobody can hear us out here. Stop being such a scaredy-wolf,' Mona replied.

Bram bit his lip and carried on walking. He thought Mona would be more careful, especially since she was the only one out of all his friends who agreed that Frostbite was up to no good. They wouldn't be able to expose him if everyone found out that they'd stolen two baby dragons from the Wicked Woods.

The campervan rumbled with a low growl as they approached.

The Cereal Killers checked their surroundings before entering, making sure they weren't being watched by anyone. Once they were all in, Mona bolted the door shut behind them.

The room was pitch-black and filled with the sounds of snoring, but a faint blue glow flickered in the far corner. Sitting there, with his arms crossed as if he had all the time in the world, was Felix Frostbite.

Frost grew around him, spreading like a halo of doom across the walls of the campervan. It crept up the Cereal Killers' bodies and glued them in place, freezing their limbs to the spot like statues.

The teacher's eyes blazed menacingly. 'The question is,' he said, looking around at each of the friends, 'why do you have two dragons in your campervan?'

CHAPTER 8
A SPARK IN THE DARK

Bram screamed, pure terror filling him as the dragon master lurked in the corner. But as his eyes flicked to Alfonso and Jaxon – who were somehow still sleeping soundly – he was glad that he and Mona had saved them from the Wicked Woods. He would do it again in a heartbeat, even if it meant Frostbite was going to report the Cereal Killers to the school, or even worse, *destroy* them.

'You've all been *very* bad. And not the good type of bad,' Frostbite said, stretching his legs. 'Where did you find these dragons?'

'None of your business,' Mona replied bluntly. 'Now, if you don't mind, please unfreeze us and get off our property.'

'Oh, no, no, no. That's not how this is about to play out. You're going to tell me what you're up to or else . . .'

Mona rolled her eyes. 'Only if you tell us what you're up to first.'

Frostbite grinned. 'I think you already know my plans, don't you, Miss Smartypants? Ever since Bram saw my map a few weeks ago, I've been watching you all to see what you were going to do.'

'And what are your plans, exactly?' Mona said, trying to coax a confession out of the teacher.

'Yes, why have you got a map of the Wicked Woods with the words "DRAGONS" and "DESTROY" written on it?' Bram joined in.

Sheila, Tony and Bryan remained silent, realization finally dawning on them.

'*None of your business*,' Frostbite mocked. 'I'm bored of you all already. If you're not going to tell me why you have these dragons and how you got them, then you're no use to me. Have a nice time trying to break out of the frost whilst I take what's rightfully mine,' he said as he stood up and stroked Jaxon down his spine.

'Don't touch them!' Bram shouted. He couldn't stand the thought of what Frostbite might do with the baby dragons, and even though they were always chewing his toes and had almost burnt off his eyebrows, he'd become very fond of them. 'They're not yours to take! What are you planning to do with them?'

'It's simple really. I'm going to steal all the dragons from Villains Academy and then I'm going to destroy the world!' Frostbite cackled.

Sheila gasped. 'You're a horrible man!'

'Ouchie,' Frostbite said sarcastically. 'You all fell for my charming dragon-master façade and didn't think twice about my ulterior motives. Now my plans are in motion and nobody suspects me, apart from you meddling kids. All that's left for me to do is steal the dragons and then I'll be unstoppable. Pity, because I like a good fight.'

'We're going to stop you,' Bram threatened. 'You won't get away with this!'

'But I already have. I'll be gone by the time you break free from my ice prison. It's been nice knowing you. I hope you like the cold.' Frostbite wrapped his arms round the baby dragons and swooped out of the door.

Tendrils of frost and ice began to grow into solid bars inside the campervan. They criss-crossed over the door and windows, sealing the friends in.

'**NO!**' Bram shouted.

'I'm sorry,' Sheila muttered to Bram and Mona. 'We should have believed you guys.'

'I didn't realize he was so evil,' Bryan said. 'Well, I knew he was evil, but I didn't think he'd do anything like *this*.'

Tony's jaw chattered. 'S-s-s-orry.'

'Yes, you should have believed us,' Mona replied bluntly.

'It doesn't matter now,' Bram said. 'There's no point arguing amongst ourselves. Let's just move forward and focus on getting out of here and stopping Frostbite.'

The Cereal Killers all agreed to put the past behind them, which made Bram reflect on how far they'd come since they'd joined the school. Only a few months ago, they had argued non-stop, but now they were used to working as a team to achieve their goals.

The gang tried everything to escape the ice that froze them in place. Tony's head toppled off as he attempted to chew through it, which only made his brain freeze worse. Mona went to use her magic but couldn't summon it with her hands being frozen. Bryan tried melting it with a fart, which to nobody's surprise didn't work. Even Sheila, the queen of cold, couldn't fly through the ice.

All they could do was wait until it thawed.

The frost around them twinkled goodnight as their surroundings descended further into ominous darkness. Sheila wailed lullabies; Tony complained that he was missing his nightly flossing routine; Bryan fell asleep standing up. The ice slowly melted as the hours passed by, and as the early birds began to chirp and the first rays of dawn crept across the horizon, Bram felt his knees give way as the frost melted around him and his friends.

But the prison that Frostbite had locked them in was going nowhere. The bars of ice were as hard as steel and hadn't melted one drop through the night. Bram pulled on them hopelessly, desperate to escape and warn everyone beyond, but they refused to budge. Sheila ricocheted off the walls as she tried to fly through them, and Bryan attempted to climb through the vent in the roof, but that was sealed just as tight.

'We're doomed,' Sheila wailed. 'We're all *doomed*!'

'Oh, will you *shut up*?' Mona snapped. 'That isn't going to help anyone.'

'We have to find a way to get out of here. The school needs to be warned about Frostbite's evil plan before it's too late,' Bram said.

'No,' Mona replied. 'We can't tell the whole school, only Master Mardybum. Nobody else will believe us whilst they're still under Frostbite's spell, but Mardybum will. He's the only one that hates Frostbite as much as we do.'

'Fine, but we need to escape from here first. And in case you've all forgotten, our exam is this morning. I am *not* missing my chance to attend the Blizzard Bash because of this. So if we could chop-chop,' Tony added.

'Missing the Blizzard Bash wouldn't be the worst thing in the world.' Mona shrugged. 'But I'm working on a plan to break us out.' She flexed her fingers and shot magic at the ice bars sealing the door. Blinding blue sparks bounced off and burst like a firework around the campervan. The bars didn't yield, but where the magic had struck them, a tiny crack had started to form.

'I'm not good enough,' Mona sighed. 'My power will never work against a villain like Frostbite.'

'You *are* good enough!' Bram said, rushing to Mona's side. She was one of the most talented villains he'd met at Villains Academy, and he desperately wanted her to realize that. 'You have more power in your pinky than all four of us combined. You just need to believe in yourself. Your parents will be so proud when they find out how much you've already achieved here.' He placed a hand on her shoulder.

Sheila, Tony and Bryan all agreed and gathered around her too, pulling her into a squishy hug.

Mona's eyes glistened with tears (although if anyone had called her out on it, she would have denied it and said it was the cold). 'Thank you.' She smiled at her friends.

She turned back to grab the icy bars

and closed her eyes whilst the Cereal
Killers chanted, 'MONA, MONA,
MONA!'. Her hands began to pulsate as
sparks of magic burst around the room.
The ice beneath her hands blazed and the
campervan lit up as brightly as if they
were sitting on the surface of the sun.

Bram watched the magic rise through Mona's body and felt a thrum through his paw that still rested on her shoulder. Her hands turned deathly white and with a **BANG** that pierced the gang's eardrums, the bars shattered into tiny pieces and flew through the air with a force that swept them off their feet. Ice shards and destruction settled around them, and through a cloud of dense smoke, Mona walked out of the open door as if she had just won a war.

'Let's get out of here, Cereal Killers. We've got an exam and a dragon-master baddie to crush,' she said as she turned on her heel and stormed towards Villains Academy.

CHAPTER 9

THE TRICKY TEST

The Cereal Killers skidded in utter panic towards the library, where Master Mardybum was standing, tapping his foot impatiently.

'Master Mardybum! Thank the devil,' Bram said as he rushed over to him. 'It's Felix Frostbite, he's—'

'How many times do I have to tell you not to mention that nincompoop's name around me?' Master Mardybum interrupted as his eyes burned with fire. 'Now stop blabbering and get into that exam hall. You're the last ones to arrive and it's about to start.'

'But, sir,' Bram begged. 'You have to listen—'

'ENOUGH of your whining,' Master Mardybum snapped. 'I don't care if you're not prepared. Utter one more word and I'll zap you so you're as crisp as a burnt piece of toast.'

The clock chimed nine.

'IN,' Master Mardybum yelled and shoved them all through the door to the library.

It had been transformed into a cold and empty exam hall, its usual warm and inviting tables replaced with rows of single desks. Every footstep the gang took echoed up to the ceiling, announcing their lateness.

The examiner at the far end of the room, a shrill-looking centipede named Professor Plops, scuttled his legs towards them and screamed at them to take their seats. Beside him, angry bookworm invigilators peered over their spectacles and tapped their clipboards menacingly.

A row of desks lined the wall where all their teachers sat watching. Master Mardybum had now parked himself with his knitting, Guru Gertrude's eyes were closed as if she was about to nod off and Matron Bones mouthed obscenities at them. At the end of the row, cast in shadow, was Felix Frostbite. His piercing eyes grew wide as he watched the Cereal Killers walk to their desks, clearly wondering how they'd escaped *and* made it to the exam on time.

'SIT YOUR BOTTOMS DOWN. THE EXAM IS ABOUT TO START,'

Professor Plops screamed.

'All right, Sir Grumpy. Calm down,' Tony replied.

'There will be NO talking. There will be NO loud breathing. There will be NO chewing, chomping or clicking of pens. There may be cheating, but only if you're confident you can get away with it. Understood?' the centipede threatened.

There was a nod of understanding from the students in Class Z's year group, who all sat like statues at their desks before a deafeningly loud klaxon announced the start of the exam, making Bryan fart in fright.

'You have thirty minutes.' The centipede grinned ominously. 'Worst wishes and baddest luck.'

Bram glanced at Frostbite, then at his friends. They couldn't confront him

now, not with an exam to complete and no physical proof. He looked down at the paper on his desk and turned it over slowly, but he was so distracted by thoughts of Frostbite that the words on the page all blurred into one and his mind went blank. The questions covered everything he'd learnt at Villains Academy so far. There was one about cape-swishing, poisons, the alignment of stars and more. He frantically scribbled down what he could.

Deep down, he was terrified of failing the exam, disappointing his dads and missing out on all the fun at the Blizzard Bash. Although if Frostbite had his way, the Blizzard Bash would be the least of Villains Academy's worries. Bram desperately wanted to stop him, but he didn't know how. Not without help.

WHACK.

A piece of paper hit the side of Bram's head. He swivelled round to find Mona mouthing something at him.

'NO LOOKING AROUND. FACE THE FRONT RIGHT NOW OR I'LL PULL OFF YOUR HEAD,' shouted a bookworm and hit Bram with a ruler.

Bram twisted his neck so quick that his head almost *did* fall off. 'Sorry, I—'

'Stop being so loud and distracting, Bram,' Mal jeered across the room. 'Can I get extra time for being interrupted?'

Professor Plops moved his legs so fast towards them that it looked like he was floating. 'I'll tell you both once and once only. There are many books in this library, and they make brilliant weapons. I am not afraid to use them on you. No talking is allowed in this exam. This is your final warning or you're *out*.' The students nodded and put their heads down to complete their tests.

Shelia flicked her tail quickly, scribbling down anything she could. Tony's pinky finger flew through the air as he gripped the pen too hard. Bryan's head rolled off the table as he struggled to stay awake. The tick-tock of a clock on the wall crept into Bram's eardrums and made him shuffle in discomfort. But Mona sat peacefully with her arms crossed, staring at Frostbite. Her exam paper was unturned, and her body was motionless as she battled in the fiercest death stare of her life.

Bram noticed and tried to get

Mona's attention, but her head didn't move, so he wrote her a note and daringly launched it at her head whilst the examiners were distracted.

It said:

> What are you doing?! You can't flunk your exam just because you don't want to go to the Blizzard Bash! Frostbite isn't going anywhere right now. Complete your exam and then we'll stop him.

Mona read the note and placed it back on her desk. 'Stop distracting me,' she said with a turn of her head.

'I'm trying to help you!' Bram whispered.

'THAT'S IT!' the centipede shouted. 'YOU TWO ARE OUT OF HERE. YOU'RE ABOUT TO FEEL THE

fULL fORCE OF mY WRATH!'

The bookworms gathered around
the examiner and bundled together
as if they were a vicious army.
The teachers looked up at the
commotion, and Bram's eyes grew
wide as the invigilators advanced
on him and Mona.

'Right, I'm
not waiting any
longer. Frostbite
is going down!'
Mona said as she
threw her exam
paper into the
air and shot out
a bolt of magic
that exploded
towards the
dragon master.

But the teacher was no longer there. In the split second that everyone had been distracted, he'd slipped out of the room to complete the last stage of his evil plan.

'**Poo balls!**' Bram exclaimed. He looked down at his exam, half filled in with nonsense. Part of him was reluctant to leave it incomplete, but the other part of him, the *bad* part, didn't care. His skills couldn't be assessed fairly based on what he wrote on a certain day, at a certain time, under certain conditions, on a stupid piece of paper. Some lessons were learnt through living life to the fullest. And right now they had more urgent matters to attend to, like stopping Felix Frostbite from stealing all the dragons from Villains Academy.

'Let's get out of here.' Bram winked at his friends and tipped over his desk, sending paper and pens flying. Behind him, Sheila, Tony and Bryan joined in the chaos.

The bookworms surrounded the Cereal Killers on all sides. Professor Plops put down his clipboard and smiled, his sharp teeth poking out of his mouth. 'I'm going to show you what happens to villains who disrupt my exams,' he said.

Mona grinned. 'Oh, yeah?' She threw her hands down on the floor and a shockwave tore through the floorboards and overturned the desks around them. Centipede and bookworms went flying, along with the odd student or two. Master Mardybum cursed, screaming something inaudible at Mona as he advanced.

But the Overlords and other pupils cheered and began throwing their exam papers into the air. Sheets of paper flew around like floating butterflies, and pens shot like bullets, piercing the walls. Everyone had joined in, and a

huge, chaotic book fight commenced,
giving the Cereal Killers the perfect
opportunity to escape through the door
and dash out into the grounds of Villains
Academy unnoticed.

They followed the trail of frosty
footprints down the grass and
ventured into the Wicked Woods.

'Now what?' Bram asked
worriedly.

Mona smiled mischievously.
'Now we go hunting for our
first enemy and save
the school!'

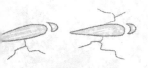

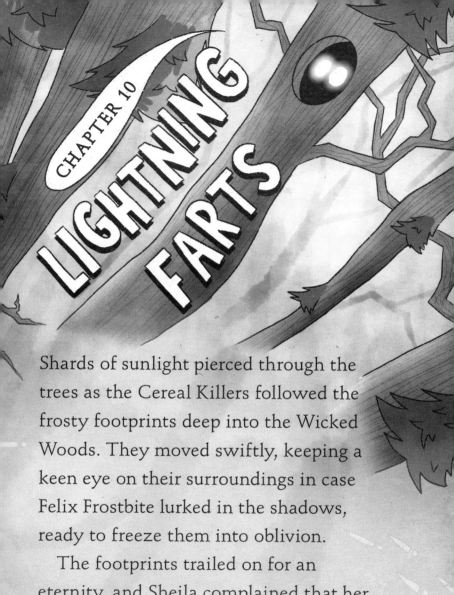

CHAPTER 10
LIGHTNING FARTS

Shards of sunlight pierced through the trees as the Cereal Killers followed the frosty footprints deep into the Wicked Woods. They moved swiftly, keeping a keen eye on their surroundings in case Felix Frostbite lurked in the shadows, ready to freeze them into oblivion.

The footprints trailed on for an eternity, and Sheila complained that her tail was hurting her.

'You're not even walking!' Tony said, frowning.

'That doesn't mean I don't use energy, bony Tony,' Sheila replied. 'It's hard work moving this gracefully.'

'*Disgracefully,*' Tony mumbled.

'Don't start.' Bryan yawned.

'Enough, all of you,' Mona said. 'Have you forgotten there are dragons and other deadly creatures in these woods? Your loud bickering will attract their attention, and I will *not* be sticking around to save your bums.'

'Touché,' Bram agreed.

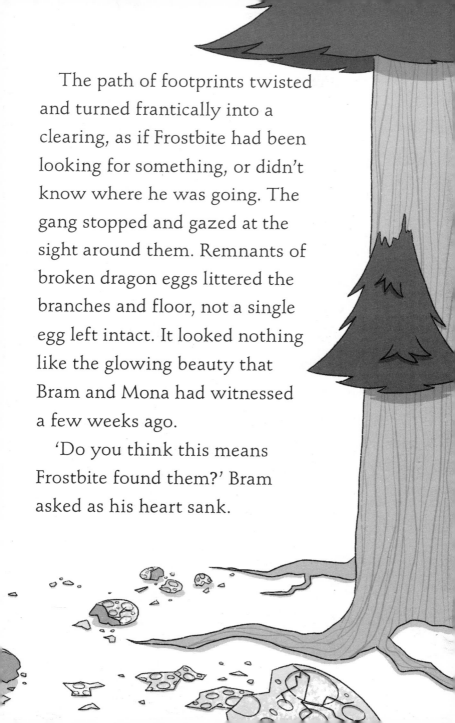

The path of footprints twisted
and turned frantically into a
clearing, as if Frostbite had been
looking for something, or didn't
know where he was going. The
gang stopped and gazed at the
sight around them. Remnants of
broken dragon eggs littered the
branches and floor, not a single
egg left intact. It looked nothing
like the glowing beauty that
Bram and Mona had witnessed
a few weeks ago.

'Do you think this means
Frostbite found them?' Bram
asked as his heart sank.

'I don't know,' Mona said, checking the discarded eggshells. 'The baby dragons may have hatched on their own and flown off. But either way, Frostbite is out here somewhere.'

'How are we going to find him?' Bryan asked.

'You're *not*,' said a voice from the trees.

Bram spun on his heels, his heart almost falling out of his mouth. The others looked around frantically, searching for the owner of the voice. But Frostbite was completely hidden from view.

Around them, a frosty chill spread through the clearing and climbed to the tips of the trees, whilst shards of ice grew from the ground and transformed into menacing frost monsters.

'Holy pepperoni!' Sheila screeched as a huge frost troll advanced on them.

The gang scattered, avoiding its fists
as they bore down into the earth where
the friends had been standing. Bram tried
his best to battle the frost monsters. He
kicked them and flicked them in the eye
as Master Mardybum had taught him,
which to his surprise actually worked.

Sheila used her tail to whip up a mini tornado that swept them away, and Tony battled them with his limbs. But every time the monsters were defeated, they came back from the dead and transformed into something else, ready to defeat the Cereal Killers.

'This isn't working,' Mona yelled, slicing off the head of a frost spider.

'No, it's really not.' Bryan cowered and let off a MASSIVE cloud of gas in fear. 'They're going to kill us!'

'Bryan, that stinks!' Sheila bawled and wafted it away. Tony recoiled in disgust, whilst Mona attempted to fan it away with her net.

The air *fizzed* with energy as she swiped at it, and she stopped in her tracks, tilting her head in curiosity. She swished her net through the air again, this time with even more force, and the cloud of methane ignited with Mona's power, sending a burst of lightning in the direction of some of the frost monsters. It tore straight through them in a loud explosion, and they didn't get back up.

'That's it!' Bram exclaimed, his eyes widening with an idea. 'Mona, ignite more of Bryan's farts.'

Bryan was happy to oblige and quickly let another one rip. As the methane escaped from his bum, Mona ignited it, sending another strike of lightning towards more of the frost monsters.

'LIGHTNING FARTS!' Tony shouted in glee. 'TAKE THAT, FROSTBITE!'

'BONKERS!' Sheila whooped.

'I'm genuinely speechless.' Bram laughed.

'Get behind us,' Mona ordered her friends as she steadied herself for a fight. Bram, Sheila and Tony gathered behind her and Bryan watched in awe. Lightning farts fired around the clearing, destroying the frost monsters in seconds.

PEW

PANG

PRRRP

POP

PRRUURRRRPPP

The final lightning fart was humongous and erupted through the clearing, melting every piece of frost left in the woods.

'YES!' Mona shouted and high-fived Bryan. '*That* was the most awesome thing we've ever done.'

'WHOOP!' Sheila cheered and hugged her friends. 'From now on, you shall be referred to as Sir Farticus, Bryan.'

Bryan yawned. 'I will absolutely not. Bryan is just fine.'

'All right, fartypants.' Sheila grinned.

'Guys, did anyone see where Frostbite went?' Bram asked, anxiously.

The Cereal Killers checked their surroundings, but there was no sign of the teacher, and suddenly the clearing sounded silent . . . Too silent.

A split second later, the head of a

GINORMOUS, terrifying dragon appeared
above them with its jaws wide open, ready
to eat them.

CHAPTER 11

ICE SCREAM

'YOU'RE A VEGETARIAN!'

Sheila screeched.

'DON'T BE A CHEAT AND EAT US!'

The dragon's jaws halted, and its eye blinked, assessing them. Then it laughed, sending a rumble echoing through the trees. 'You're funny,' it said. 'Most people scream in terror when they see me.'

'Screaming is for important things only, like having fun. I'm Sheila, by the way. Nice to meet you.'

'Pleasure, Sheila,' the dragon replied. 'I'm Bridget. Did you steal my children? Because if you did, then I'm afraid I *might* have to eat you.'

'No, we didn't,' Bram interrupted, trying to stop his whole body from shaking as the giant dragon stared into his soul. 'But I think we know who did.'

'Yes, our wacky teacher,' Sheila agreed and patted the dragon on the head. 'He's a bit of a freaky frozen fruitcake. But we don't know where he's gone.'

'We can help you, though,' Mona said.

Her body was rigid, and her eyes were as wide as flying saucers. Bram had never seen her nervous, but now he knew her limits – a massive, menacing dragon. A part of him was happy that she didn't feel the need to hide how she was feeling. Maybe she was finally comfortable being her true self around her friends.

'Okay,' Bridget said. 'If you help me find my children I won't eat you.'

'DEAL!' Sheila shouted.

'Is that the freaky frozen fruitcake?' Bridget asked as the gang lurked in the shadows of the trees.

They'd followed the frost trail further into the woods until they'd come upon a frozen fortress where Felix Frostbite stood surrounded by a mass of sleeping adult and baby dragons.

'I know you're there,' Frostbite said. His voice pierced through the quiet like a shard of ice. 'You're not being very subtle about your presence. I have to say I'm surprised you managed to get past my frost monsters back there. Maybe I did underestimate you children. Not that it matters anyway, as I'll be out of here very soon.'

Bram stepped out of the clearing, his heart beating ten to the dozen. He wasn't going to stand by whilst Frostbite stole the evilest creatures on earth away from his home. Because that's what Villains Academy had become to him – his second home, complete with newfound friends.

'The jig is up, Frostbite. There are others on their way now. You won't get away with this,' he said with as much confidence as he could muster.

Frostbite laughed. A sarcastic, painful cackle that splintered through Bram. 'And they sent you first as their heavy men, did they? Oh, Bram, you are a pathetic villain. Do you really think that you, five fledgling villains, are capable of stopping me? It's too late. I've already got away with it.' Frostbite reached inside his cloak and pulled out a weapon.

Bram ducked to the floor in fright.

PEW. PEW. PEW.

Frostbite shot straight at Bridget the
dragon who was still standing next to the
Cereal Killers. Brown substance hit her in
the face and splattered all over the gang.

'Are those bubbles?' Tony frowned.

'Is it . . . chocolate?' Sheila asked, licking her tail.

'I feel sleepy,' Bridget muttered as she swayed dangerously and crashed to the ground with a thud.

'What have you done?' Bryan roared, trying to prise open Bridget's eyelids as she snored. 'Bridget, wake up! Come on, you lazy swine! We need your help.'

'I told you. My plan is almost complete,' Frostbite sneered. 'Whilst these dragons are sleeping, tendrils of ice will wedge deep into their brains, allowing me to control them. When they wake up, they'll pledge their allegiance to me and only me. They'll become my army, and nobody, not any of you or your pathetic teachers, will be able to stop me.'

'They're not yours to control and steal,' Bram said. 'They belong to Villains Academy, and if you want them, you bet we're going to put up one hell of a fight.'

'Actually, they don't belong to anybody,' Sheila said. 'They're free spirits.'

'Actually, I think you'll find they belong to *me*.' As Frostbite spoke his last word, he shot a sharp shard of ice out of his fingertips towards the gang. They leapt out of the way, dodging it like a bullet, and Mona fired her own magic back. The woods were illuminated by sparks of blue and green. Magic shot out in all directions and frost spread around them.

It controlled everything it touched, spreading like a vicious disease and freezing the world in place. Sheila twirled about the air, dive-bombing Frostbite with her deadly Toxic Tail Swishes. But her advances were soon scuppered as he thrust her away with a tornado of icy air. Tony circled the teacher, but his feet became glued to the floor, frost creeping up his body and turning him as rigid as stone. And

Bryan became frozen in place mid-prowl towards the dragon master, his farts going unignited as Mona continued her magic battle.

Bram crawled around the edge of the clearing, moving his hands and knees off the floor as quickly as he could so that he didn't get caught by the perilous frost. He rested by the baby dragons and thought

about what he could do to help his friends defeat their evil teacher. He didn't have any special skills or magic like Mona.

Then the baby emerald-green and sea-blue dragon, Alfonso, shifted and licked Bram's cheek, almost making him scream in fright.

'I thought you were asleep?' Bram asked in surprise.

Around him, other young dragons' eyes cracked open. Jaxon looked at Bram and sat up, then quickly threw himself back down on the floor and faked a big snore.

'Are you all pretending to be asleep

to stay safe?' Bram asked in awe. 'Did the chocolate not make you go to sleep?' The cogs in Bram's mind began to turn. Frostbite had said chocolate made dragons sleepy, but that hadn't been the case for Bram when he'd been looking after the babies in the campervan.

Alfonso attempted to nudge one of the adults awake.

'Don't worry, they'll be all right,' Bram said. 'But I'm going to need your help. We need to take Frostbite down. Can the younglings wake up and distract him so that I can help my friends?'

Alfonso, Jaxon and the others began to chirp with excitement. One by one, they stretched their wings and shot off into the sky. They roared and flapped in circles

overhead, diving towards Frostbite, who
looked utterly perplexed. Bram ran to
the side of the Cereal Killers, who were
now unfrozen thanks to Frostbite's
momentary distraction, and stood back-
to-back with them, ready to take on the
world with their new army of young
dragons.

'IMPOSSIBLE!' Frostbite screeched as
he shot more chocolate at the dragons
out of his bubble gun, which only
spurred them on.

Sheila squealed with fury, working

herself up to unleash her inner beast.
Tony removed his arm and ran at full pelt
with Bryan towards the teacher. And
Bram and Mona took their positions,
ready to take Frostbite down.

'NO!' the teacher roared and sent
a wave of frost through the clearing,
freezing everything on the ground in
place. At that exact moment, Mona and
Bram leapt through the air, dodging the
ice tendrils on the floor, and were the only
two members of the gang left unfrozen.

The Wicked Woods descended into

silence, the young dragons settling around the edges of the trees, watching the final stand-off.

'Your two put up a good fight,' Frostbite said as he circled Bram and Mona. 'You should both join me. *Together* we could take over the world.'

Bram glanced at his friend who had dropped her gaze to the floor. The offer was tempting. She was lonely and wanted nothing more than to be a famous villain to prove to her parents she was bad enough. But would she betray the Cereal Killers to achieve that?

Bram thought about losing Mona as a friend and having to finish Villains Academy without her. He thought of the future generations of villains who would have no school to enrol at if the dragons weren't here to protect it. And

he thought of his own dreams, and how
Mona and the Cereal Killers had brought
him out of his shell, allowing him to be
the best villain he could be. Mona wasn't
alone, and she never had been.

Bram reached out his hand and
intertwined his fingers with Mona's.

She raised her head and locked eyes with him. Then she looked at the Cereal Killers, a shimmering tear rolling down her cheek. Finally she stared at Felix Frostbite with a fierce glare.

'I wouldn't join you in a million years. I won't betray Villains Academy, and I won't betray my friends.'

She quickly pushed her hand into her pocket and dug around for something buried deep.

'Too bad.' Frostbite shrugged and shot out a fatal shard of ice towards them.

But Mona was just as quick, pulling out a vial that Bram quickly recognized as the fringlefang juice she'd stolen from the Poisons class, weeks before. With a grin, he realized what she was about to do and leapt out of the way.

The vial soared through the air as

Mona launched it from her hand, and Bram watched it shatter into smithereens as it collided with Frostbite's chocolate stun gun. A colossal explosion ripped through the clearing, sending Frostbite and the Cereal Killers flying off their feet as the two elements reacted and the smell of burning sprouts filled the air.

The gang whooped with glee as they pushed themselves off the ground and flexed their frost-free muscles. Frostbite lay motionless, as if knocked out and in a deep sleep, having taken the brunt of the explosion, and Bryan let off a round of victorious farts to celebrate.

Mona helped Bram up and gripped his paw. Then, with a wicked grin, she raised their hands and ignited the air around them with magic. Bryan's methane sparked into life and sent a dome of lightning around the clearing, sizzling away the frost.

'Never underestimate a pathetic fledgling villain,' Mona said sarcastically, brushing her hands together in good riddance.

The dragons emerged through the smoke and gathered around the friends.

Bridget thanked them all for saving her children, as Alfonso, Jaxon and three others gathered next to her.

'I have a question,' Bram said. 'Why doesn't chocolate make baby dragons sleepy?'

'Their immune system can tolerate it at a young age,' Bridget said. 'But even the tiniest bit of chocolate is enough to send me and the other grown-up dragons into a deep sleep.'

Bridget embraced them all in a squishy hug, and Bram wondered how he'd ever been terrified by the creature.

'We should get out of here and leave you in peace,' Bram said, brushing down his woolly jumper. 'Thank you for everything you do to protect Villains Academy.'

'Any time.' Bridget smiled. 'The least

we can do after everything you've done for us is take you back to school. And I'm sure you don't want to have to carry *him* by yourselves.' She gestured at Frostbite's motionless body, loud snores escaping from his mouth.

Alfonso wandered over to Bram and nudged him lovingly with his nose. Bram looked around at his friends and beamed.

'C'mon, gang. Let's fly.'

CHAPTER 12
THE BLIZZARD BASH

WooHooooo

The Cereal Killers soared through the air towards Villains Academy, their Winter Warts training finally paying off. Each one of them let a young dragon choose them, which made riding much easier because they'd formed a bond.

Mona flew gracefully on Jaxon with Frostbite tied behind her, his strong wings beating beside them. Sheila screamed at her dragon to 'GO FASTER!',

which only made it like her more. It was
as white as snow and almost became
invisible as it blended in with the clouds.
Tony's was thin and skeletal, its slim
frame darting like a bullet through the
air. Bryan's was enormous and clumsy,
and even a little farty, which spurred
him quickly through the sky. And Bram's
dragon, Alfonso, was calm and quiet.
Its green-and-blue feathered scales were
iridescent and its teeth poked out with a
smile as Bram stroked its head.

He'd never felt so happy in his life as the wind whipped through his ears and the Wicked Woods whizzed by beneath him. He and his friends had defeated their first enemy together *and* they were riding dragons. Bram smiled. If he was bad enough to ride a dragon, he was bad enough to do anything.

Master Mardybum looked dumbfounded as he watched the Cereal Killers land their dragons outside his office window. He rushed out on to the grounds quicker than you could say *shubblemegump* and ordered them to explain what on earth was going on.

Patiently, the Cereal Killers recounted the events of last night and this morning.

'Well, I'm glad you destroyed that clown,' Master Mardybum said. 'He was so arrogant and irritating. I should have realized there was something more sinister below the surface. You've all done Villains Academy proud today. We'll take care of things from here.'

'Thank you, sir,' Bram replied, feeling pleased. 'Does this mean we're allowed to go to the Blizzard Bash after all?'

'Stop with your manners already.' Master Mardybum frowned. 'You really upset Professor Plops this morning. In fact, I think you might have made an enemy there. But, yes, I suppose you all deserve to attend the ball. I don't think I could say no after you saved the school from the clutches of an evil villain. And I was actually *very* impressed by the chaos you caused in the exam hall, but don't tell the bookworms that. Now go and get your glad rags on. The Blizzard Bash is not a party you want to miss.' He winked.

Mona sighed at the thought of having to go to the ball, but the rest of the gang had massive grins on their faces.

Bram wondered if Master Mardybum would be kinder to them now that they'd proved themselves.

'Oh, and one last thing before you go, Mona,' Master Mardybum said. 'The magic you summoned in the Wicked Woods sounded very impressive. Impressive enough to deserve the Villain of the Week title.'

Mona beamed from ear to ear. 'Me? Villain of the Week?'

'Yes. You surprised me, and I like surprises.'

'Thank you!' Mona said, her eyes shining with gratitude.

'HOW MANY TIMES?! DO NOT USE YOUR MANNERS AT ME!'

Master Mardybum roared.

The dragons fled into the sky, and the Cereal Killers shot into Villains Academy before they could feel their teacher's wrath.

'Can you believe Guru Gertrude was talking sense for once in our last Astrology lesson?' Bram said as he chose an outfit for the Blizzard Bash.

'Yes,' Sheila said seriously. 'That woman is a *genius*.'

'But just the other day you convinced her she'd marry Frostbite at the party?' Tony replied.

'Well . . .' Sheila contemplated. 'She's a genius *sometimes*. Anyway, speaking of the Blizzard Bash, are we all ready to go?'

'I told you I'm not coming,' Mona moaned.

Just a few moments earlier, Sheila had attempted to put Mona in a glittery dress, which had made her so furious she'd almost pulled off Sheila's tail. Tony had offered to teach Mona to dance, reassuring her that nobody would look her way if she was stood next to a skeleton with no rhythm. And Bryan had even suggested riding her into the party on his back as a grand entrance, to which she muttered something obscene.

'Mona,' Bram said, sitting down beside her on her bed. This was his last chance to pluck up the courage to ask her to the ball. 'Will you come to the Blizzard Bash

with me? Everyone has a skill they're no
good at, and it just so happens that yours
is dancing, but I can help you – we all
can. You don't even have to dance if you
don't want to. We just don't want you to
miss out.'

Mona glanced around the room,
clearly torn, but the Cereal Killers
beamed at her in response and Bram
turned on his best puppy-dog eyes.

'Fine,' Mona mumbled and began rummaging through her drawers for something to wear. 'But if Sheila comes near me with that dress one more time, I'm going to throttle you all.'

'Fair enough.' Sheila shrugged.

'Fabulous!' Bram beamed in his best knitted jumper. It had flashing lights around down the seams and sparkly thread woven throughout.

Tony wore a bedazzling mirrorball cape, Bryan brushed his mane and donned a bowtie and Sheila covered herself in glitter, whilst Mona put on her best hat, shiny shoes and velvet jumpsuit that was embroidered with the words GO AWAY.

'Oh, glitterchops. You all look fabulous!' Sheila said. 'Let's go, Cereal Killers.'

The gang walked through the halls of
Villains Academy and out to the grounds.
In the distance, under the stars, the
school had come out in full force ready
to party. Food and drink stands had been
erected, filled with delicious snacks and
tantalizing treats. Bunting, fairy lights
and dazzling glitterballs hung on the
trees of the Wicked Woods, swaying in
the cool evening breeze like fireflies.

Music blared and crowds of people danced on the huge dance floor in the middle of the grass.

Guru Gertrude wore a wedding dress and searched through the crowd for her beloved Felix Frostbite who was being locked up for his crimes, unbeknown to the rest of Villains Academy who were being kept in the dark about the whole ordeal.

At the edge of the woods, a stage had been built, and ominous mist crawled out from the treeline. Bram could have sworn he saw the eyes of a dragon peering out from within it, and he smiled at the thought of them dancing to the music.

'Your powers have got so strong now,' Bram said to Mona, trying to make conversation as they walked through the crowd.

'I know,' Mona replied. 'It's because of you guys.'

'*Us?*' Bram asked, confused.

'Yes.' Mona smiled. 'You're my family now and I can feel the love I have for each of you coursing through my veins. That's how I defeated Frostbite – with the power of love.'

Bram's eyes glistened with tears. 'That's beautiful, Mona. I hope you know that we love you too.'

'I know.' Mona beamed. 'But never tell anyone I just said that, or I'll have to kill you.'

'Never.' Bram grinned back and motioned zipping his mouth closed.

A low rumble echoed through the microphone and dazzling spotlights illuminated the stage as a buzz of electrifying excitement rippled through the throng of students.

'FOR ONE NIGHT, AND ONE NIGHT ONLY, WE GIVE YOU . . .

THE SOUL SISTERS!'

a voice boomed through the speakers, but it was soon drowned out by the crowd's ear-splitting screams as four of the most fabulous villains emerged on to the stage.

The Cereal Killers gawped at the band with their mouths wide open.

Sheila almost fainted, Tony's jaw fell off and rolled through the crowd and Bryan let off a quiet fart. Mona grabbed Bram's paw and squeezed hard.

'NO WAY!' she said with her eyes fixed on one figure in the centre of the stage.

'Holy pepperoni, macaroni *and* cannelloni!' Sheila screeched. 'Is that Master Mardybum?!'

Their form teacher stood on stage with the Soul Sisters, his friendship group from his schooldays at Villains Academy, and posed in a long, glittery gown that was covered from head to toe in sequins. Confident and uncaring, he strutted towards the crowd with his sisters, held his microphone high and began to sing 'Dancing Scream'.

Bram couldn't help but grin.

Villains were always full of surprises.

'Care to dance?' Bram asked as he squeezed Mona's hand back.

'I don't know how to,' she replied, a pink tinge growing on her cheeks.

'Like this,' Tony shouted and began jiggling his bones up and down like he had in Frostbite's office. The crowd went wild, backing up to make room for Tony to bust his moves.

'THE BRAIN FREEZE BOOGIE!' Sheila screeched as the other students began to copy him. 'OH, TONY, YOU'RE A TRENDSETTER!'

Mona laughed. The Cereal Killers and the rest of the crowd began shimmying up and down as if they all had terrible brain freeze like Tony.

Bram danced beside Mona and encouraged her to do whatever felt natural. Their arms waved all over the place and neither of them looked cool, but he didn't care. He was just thankful to be surrounded by his favourite misfits in the whole world. And they weren't just his friends any more, they were his chosen family, and he couldn't have asked for anyone better.

Bram took Mona's hand and began to wiggle his hips to Master Mardybum's high notes. It felt good to let go of the worries and stresses of being a villain. Sometimes all you needed was to have a little bit of fun – being evil could wait until later.

ACKNOWLEDGEMENTS

Writing *Villains Academy: How to Steal a Dragon* was quite different to writing the first book. I wrote that one in the attic of my parents' house and never expected anyone else to read it. I wrote the second book as I juggled moving into my own home, getting a puppy, balancing a full-time job and illustrating the insides of book one, whilst trying to stay somewhat sane. I've poured so much love and fun into these books, and I will never tire of writing about my villains' antics. I adore them and could write about them for ever. I hope you enjoyed their latest adventure!

Thank you as always to my magnificent agent, Lydia. I'm glad you liked Bryan's lightning farts. Thank you for encouraging my silliness and for always being so supportive.

Thank you to the incredible team at S&S – you're all beyond badass, and I can't thank you enough. To my editors, the devilish duo, Amina and Ali, for putting up with my many emails and wacky ideas, you're both true evil gems.

To my designer Sean for being supportive and patient with my creative ideas. To my marketer and publicist, Dan and Ellen, you're both the most incredible and creative people – thank you for everything. Thank you to Maud in the rights team for getting these villains into kids' hands across the world, in all languages, shapes and sizes! And for everyone in between who works so hard behind the scenes. Making a book is a massive team effort, so thank you to every single one of you.

Thank you to my family. To Mum and Dad, who continuously support and encourage me to follow my dreams (and try to hand-sell my books to everyone they meet). I'm forever grateful to you both. To Nicola, Brad, Gracie, Caron, Martin, Jim and Maureen – thank you for being the best family and for accepting me as I am.

Thank you to my partner-in-crime, Mitch. I'm sorry for ignoring you and zoning out into the world of Villains Academy most evenings. I'm lucky to have someone as supportive and loving as you. These books wouldn't be what they are without you. Love you lots.

To my brother, Jamie, to whom the book is dedicated. Thank you for making us cry with

laughter by creating the word *shubblemegump* –
I will never forget that moment. So much of our
childhood laughter and imagination has fed into
this series, and I'm forever thankful for that. All
that time spent playing with LEGO and making
stories has paid off. Now we just need LEGO
versions of the Cereal Killers!

Thank you to Luke for your love of ABBA
(Master Mardybum's alter ego is especially for you.
I hope you enjoyed that scene). And to your dog,
Jaxon, who has a very small cameo as a dragon.

To my dog, Alfonso. You're top of the
naughty list and cause much more destruction
than a dragon ever could, but I wouldn't change
you for the world. Thank you for your chaos,
feet-biting and constant kisses.

Thank you to my friends. To Emily for being
as excitable as Sheila. To Lowri for being so
kind and supportive. To Anna for your shared
love of books. To Hannah and Sarah for your
adorable dogs and many years of friendship. To
Sarah L for Rhianna Von Flippleflapple and silly
email sign-offs. And to Lois for dressing up as
Mona on World Book Day! To Asmaa for being
hilarious and talking as much as I do. To Lins,
and more importantly, Seth – my first proper
reader! And to everyone else that my terrible

memory has forgotten, thank you for giving my life so much joy.

Thank you to my fellow authors and illustrators. I can't tell you how much your kindness and support means to me. You're truly the best bunch of people and are changing the lives of children one book at a time.

Thank you to the booksellers, teachers, librarians and adult and child readers who have entered into Villains Academy and shouted about it from the rooftops. You're the true stars of the show, and I couldn't do any of this without your incredible support.

A big thank you to my primary school teacher, Miss Loxley, who had a photograph of Alan Rickman in her store cupboard and screamed at it when she was frustrated at her students. You're a total legend and completely inspired Master Mardybum's meltdown.

As always, thank you to Sheila the real-life ghost. I hope you follow me wherever I go in life.

And finally, thank you to *you* for reading this book. You're as much a part of the Cereal Killers as I am, and remember, being a little bit bad can be a good thing. Go destroy your enemies with love and live your best life.

WHO IS RYAN HAMMOND?

Ryan Hammond is an author, illustrator and book designer. He likes quirky characters, nature, dragons and VILLAINOUS streaks.

He currently lives in Sheffield in an extremely haunted house, surrounded by lots and LOTS of books. **Villains Academy** was his first book.

HOW TO DRAW BRAM

1.

Draw a circle.

2.

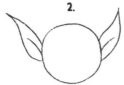

Add ears.

3.

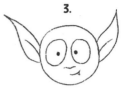

Add eyes, a nose and a mouth.

4.

Add the swirls of Bram's hair.

5.

Add strands of hair below the swirls.

6.

Add fur all over.

7.

Draw a body and arms.

8.

Add legs, feet and hands.

9.

Colour in for a woolly jumper effect!

HOW TO DRAW MONA

1.

Draw a circle.

2.

Draw two smaller
circles for eyes.

3.

Add pupils, eyelids,
a nose and a mouth.

4.

Draw ears and
add earrings.

5.

Add a fringe.

6.

Draw an oval for the
top of Mona's hat.

7.

Draw the point of her hat
and a 'GO AWAY' badge.

8.

Add a body.

9.

Draw her arms
crossed.

10.

Add legs, feet and
long hair.

11.

Colour in for extra
grumpiness!

HOW TO DRAW BRYAN

1.

Draw Bryan's face shape – make sure it's wider at the bottom for his furry chin.

2.

Add his nose.

3.

Add eyes and a mouth.

4.

Draw his fluffy mane.

5.

Draw his front legs and arch of his back.

6.

Add his back legs so he's sitting down.

7.

Add his tail and colour in – don't forget his furry texture!

HOW TO DRAW SHEILA (X2)

1.

2.

3.

Draw a shape that tails off – any shape, Sheila is really flexible!

Add two circles for eyes.

Add a mouth and two smaller circles inside the first two to give her the hollow-eye look!

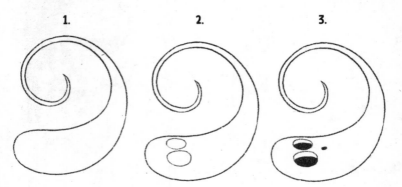

1.

2.

3.

Draw a shape that tails off – any shape, Sheila is really flexible!

Add two circles for eyes.

Add a mouth and two smaller circles inside the first two to give her the hollow-eye look!

HOW TO DRAW TONY

1.

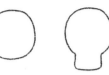

Draw a
circle.

2.

Add a rectangle
underneath for
his jaw.

3.

Add eyes, a nose
and a mouth.

4.

Draw a circle
around his head
for his hood.

5.

Add horns!

6.

Draw the front two
strands of his cape
and add a button.

7.

Add his arms,
ribs and hips.

8.

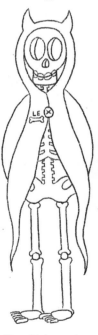

Draw his legs and
feet – remember
they are bones!

9.

Colour in for extra
spookiness!

LOOK OUT FOR MORE
EVIL ADVENTURES IN . . .

VILLAINS ACADEMY

HOW TO WIN THE GRUESOME GAMES

COMING
APRIL 2024!

Be Bad